Daffodil Days

Stories from Broome Park Prefab Village

(A Fabrian Book)

Pat Posner

Typesetting and Design Fabrian Books – fabrianbooks.com.

Cover Illustration: David Young - http://www.davidyoungillustration.co.uk

Welcome to Broome Park Prefab Village

Step back in time to the early 1950s when the aftermath of World War Two was still etched deeply in memories, some foods were still on ration, menfolk were on – or returning from – National Service and Britain was about to crown a new queen.

This collection of stories is about the families who live in Broome Park Prefab Village. Stories of friendship, good neighbours, a war widow whose young daughter wishes for a Daddy, love and romance, a very special Christmas, shared problems and the occasional crime.

About the Author

Pat started out writing children's fiction published by Bloomsbury, Hodder, Egmont and Scholastic.

Nowadays she writes contemporary romance and stories of family, friendship and love set in the 1950s published by DC Thomson, Ulverscroft and Fabrian Books.

Pat lives in a farmhouse on a sheep farm with her husband. They are owned by Tim and Ted, their 2 Rough Collies, visiting wildlife and the sheep who graze in the moorland meadows outside Pat's study window.

My love to my husband, Peter, who never fails to support and encourage me.

Daffodil Days

"Maisie. Maisie, we've got a letter from the Housing Department."

Turning from stirring a large pan of porridge, for it was her turn to make breakfast and get the children off to school, Maisie watched her husband weave his way through nieces and nephews and their own three daughters – Dilly the eldest and the seven-year-old twins. Andy was reading the letter and, from the look on his face, Maisie knew it must be good news.

It was almost ten years to the day since a bomb had destroyed their home. With Andy in the army and overseas at the time and their first baby due in a few weeks, Maisie had come to live, alongside her two married sisters and sister-in-law and their babies, in her parents' terraced house. It had been worrying times for all of them.

There'd been bright moments though. After receiving the telegram announcing his daughter's birth, Andy had managed to get a friend on leave to deliver Maisie a bunch of daffodils, her favourite flowers because they symbolised "The promise of eternal life". That was when Maisie had decided to call their baby Dilys. She'd be Dilly for short, like Daffy-down-Dilly. Dilly and the flowers had brought hope for the future to all the family.

Andy joined them when the war ended and he was de-mobbed and Maisie put their names on the re-housing list. That was near on eight years ago. All this time of feeling like a sardine in a tin, Maisie mused as Andy, dodging a flailing elbow, got closer to her. Not that she'd seen a tin of sardines for ages; instead there was snoek or barracuda. Whatever, it now seemed that living almost literally side by side with so many relations was about to come to an end.

Maisie felt a spurt of excitement. Even Dilly's plaintive: "Mum, Pauline is wearing *my* liberty bodice," didn't deter Maisie from grabbing the letter from Andy's hand.

"You put Pauline's on then," she told Dilly. Dilly's cousin was the same age and size. "It's there, warming on the fireguard. And be quick about it, Dilly. I don't know why you always have to be the last one to get dressed," she added impatiently, before quickly scanning the contents of the letter.

"But where is Knott Lane?" she asked Andy, pointing to the address of the house allocated to them. "I've never heard of it." As much as she wanted them to have a home of their own, she wanted it to be near her large family. Andy's job meant he worked shifts and she needed company when he was working in the evening.

"It's probably somewhere off the main road, so you..." Andy broke off and sniffed. "I think the porridge is burning, Maisie."

"And, Auntie Maisie, we'll miss the school bus if we don't start eating breakfast now," said one of the nephews. With her attention back on the pan of porridge, Maisie wasn't sure which of the four boys had spoken.

"Get them fed and off, love," Andy said. "Where's my bicycle clips? I'll go and collect the key from the Council Office. Should be back for half-nine and I'm not due at work until two so we'll have time to go and look at the house."

The children left soon after Andy. The kitchen was soon full again, though, as Maisie's parents, her brother and sister-in-law and her younger sister, Dot, came to get their breakfasts.

Maisie told them about the letter. "Andy's gone to fetch the key," she added as her mum spooned tea leaves into a large brown teapot.

"Good thing tea's off ration, our Maisie. Shame sugar isn't yet but we can celebrate with a good strong cuppa and I think I might have a tin of condensed milk in the sideboard. Mind, I'm not sure you, Andy and the girls leaving us *is* a reason to celebrate."

"Oh, it is," Dot said with a grin. "Me and my lot can have their attic room. But we'll really miss you, Maisie."

Maisie shook her head. "You won't be getting rid of me that easy. "I'll be calling in every day."

"Either that, else we'll all come to yours," said her mum pouring out the tea.

*

"We need the number eighteen bus and we get off the stop before Broome Park, Maisie," Andy told her.

"Not that far away then," Maisie said with relief.

But it took fifteen minutes to get to the stop they needed.

"Nothing will take as long when there's no fog," Andy said as, ten minutes after getting off the bus, he and Maisie made their way down a road with what looked like large huts with flat roofs just visible on either side. "Prefabs," Andy told her. "Temporary homes, they are."

Maisie, dismayed at the length of the walk from the bus stop and how far this already was from her parents' house and from any shops, wondered, fog or no fog, how much longer it would be until they reached Knott Lane. And would their house be one of these prefabs or would it be a proper house like they lived in now?

Another few minutes went by before they came to a turning. Maisie bent to look at the name plate. "Yes, this is it." Straightening, she made her hands into binoculars and peered down the lane. She could just make out, right at the far end, four similar buildings to those they'd passed; two either side of the lane with, she thought, a grass area in the middle.

"The prefabs along the road have been there about five years," Andy said. "I remember passing them on the train when I was porter at Blakeley Station. But I think these have only recently been put up. Council must have purchased a bit more land, else had four left over and decided to put them here."

"It'll be like living in the countryside," Maisie said. Even in the fog she could see it had once been a large field, though they were walking on a pavement and there were a couple of lamp posts. The countryside was all right for a day out, but living in it would be a different matter. She'd miss the comings and goings you got on a street with lots of houses and people. Worst of all, it was too far away for her to see her family that often. Once a week if she were lucky.

Number one was right at the very end with gardens at either side and the front and the back as well. "Even if we're moved on in a few years, we've hit the jackpot here, Maisie, with the park right next to the side garden. I reckon the back overlooks parkland, too. The girls are going to love it."

Oh, heck, Maisie thought. *He sounds really enthusiastic*. "You can't call any of this a garden as such," she replied waving a hand towards brambles and dead bushes and grass. "And anyway, Andy, I'm not right sure this–"

“Come on, let’s hurry and go in.” Andy nudged Maisie gently up the path that led to the front door. “I’ve heard folks say prefabs are like little palaces inside.”

*

Maisie had to admit it was nice. “So much space,” she said. “And so many cupboards and drawers. There’s even big cupboards for clothes in both bedrooms. And an indoor toilet in a room on its own and a bathroom.

“The floors need a right good scrubbing,” she continued, “and we’ll have to stain them and get some carpet squares. The windows want cleaning as well. I’ll run up some curtains, I’ll be able to get back to my sewing, there’s plenty of room for my treadle machine and laying out patterns and such. And Mum and Dot and Joan and Vivian are going to be so jealous when they see this kitchen. We’ve even got a fridge.”

“So.” Andy grinned at her, “Even though it won’t be our *Forever Home* you think this will do?”

She wasn’t really sure. “It’s a fair distance away from Mum and Dad’s but I suppose everyone can come over on the bus a time or two and spend the day here.”

“If you could get a bit of sewing work, we can save up and get you and the girls a bike each, Maisie. You could ride over and see the family quite often then.”

Maisie nodded. But it would take a while before they’d saved enough. How would she go on ’til then?

*

During the following week, Maisie’s sisters and sister-in-law helped with the scrubbing and cleaning, then Andy and her brother Bernard stained the wooden floors. A small Trojan removal van brought their beds and other bits of furniture and now, on another foggy day, number one Knott Lane was ready and waiting for them.

Apart from the day we came together to see it, this will be the first time Andy and I have been alone here, thought Maisie as they walked towards the front door. *It's going to feel strange.*

Andy was working nights but he'd swapped shifts with one of the other station porters so he could spend all day and the night in their new home. The three girls had gone to school as usual. They'd be catching a different school bus at home time, though, and would be dropped off at the end of the lane.

Smiling, Andy swept Maisie into his arms and carried her over the threshold. When he put her down in the hallway she glanced at the dark-stained wooden floor and the carpet runner she'd found at a jumble sale. "Looks good, doesn't it?" she said trying to feel positive about things as she walked towards the living room.

She stopped in the doorway and gasped with real pleasure when she saw a huge bunch of daffodils in a jug on the small table Andy had made out of wooden bread trays. How she loved this man of hers. *And how guilty she felt for missing her family already.*

"Not picked from someone's garden this time, Maisie," Andy said as they walked over to the table together. Except for the very first time, and that time in the war, Andy always said that when he gave her daffodils. She'd only been six and Andy eight when he'd first presented her with some. She remembered her delight – followed quickly by fright when Andy admitted he'd picked them from a neighbour's garden. She'd tried to make him put them back but, of course, he couldn't. Instead, they'd both gone round to confess and apologise and had to run errands for weeks to pay for the flowers.

"Now," Andy said, obviously guessing Maisie's thoughts, "I think you'll have to pay me for them."

Maisie reached up to kiss him and it was quite a while before she recovered enough to suggest they should have their first elevensies snack in their new home.

*

"So, Maisie," said her mum two weeks later, "are you happy to be living here? You've certainly got it looking homely and cosy," she added. "You made a right good job of the curtains, hang beautifully, they do."

Maisie nodded.

"The girls settling in all right, are they?"

"Linda and Dinah have settled a treat. They love it. Dilly's finding it hard, though. The twins have got each other but Dilly misses having all her cousins around. She's lonely without them, Mum."

"And you know just how Dilly feels."

Maisie knew it wasn't a question. Her mum had always been able to read her like a book. "Oh, Mum, I love Andy and the girls and I love our prefab. I just wish we were nearer to you. I'm like a single pea in a pod rattling around on my own most of the day with only the wireless for company."

Maisie sighed. "Hearing voices coming from that even make me feel worse at times. It might be real folk talking but they don't answer when I talk back, I can't touch them, ask them to get out of my way. Can't pour them a cuppa..."

"It will–"

"Don't tell me it will get better. That's what Andy says. You know, apart from seeing the milkman every day and the grocer and baker when their vans stop at the corner of the lane, I hardly ever see anyone else, not even when I walk up or down Blakeley Road where all the other prefabs are. Sometimes I get a bus to the nearest shops even when I don't need anything. At least I can talk to whoever sits near me and to other shoppers."

"Winter's almost at an end, Maisie. The weather's getting better and it won't be long before folk are out and about more. You'll make friends then, love, and you'll likely have neighbours soon. They won't keep the other three places empty for long."

"I suppose it will be better once others come to live on the lane. At least I'd *see* other humans then. And, hopefully, there'll be someone with a daughter or even a son around Dilly's age."

"Bound to be," her mum agreed. "Any more tea in that pot? I'm still parched after the long walk from the bus stop."

Maisie jumped up. "I'll make another pot. I've no more sugar to spare though, Mum. Just enough of the ration left for the breakfast tomorrow."

"No matter." Her mum smiled and dipped into the large handbag that went everywhere with her. "I brought lollipops for the children. They won't know there's one short if we use it to stir our tea."

Maisie blinked away a tear. It was the silly little things like that she missed the most – sharing and solving problems.

Her mum stayed for another hour and then Maisie walked her to the bus stop. On her way back a couple of women smiled at her and said "Hello". Maybe her mum was right and there would be more people about now the weather was on the turn. The thought cheered Maisie up a bit and she decided to make Spam and potato fritters, Dilly's favourite, for tea; that might make Dilly feel more cheerful, too.

*

The next day dawned bright and sunny. "I'll be home by four," Andy said before hurrying off to work. "If the weather stays this good, I'll put an hour or two in on the side garden."

"I might have a go at clearing the back," Dilly said. "There's nothing else for me to do round here."

Maisie sighed, knowing Dilly's loneliness matched her own. "We'll have your cousins over to stay for a weekend soon," she said. "Gran and I talked about that yesterday. You can start making plans when you see them at school. But you need to leave to catch the bus now else you won't *get* there."

After making the beds and tidying around, Maisie decided to start making frocks for the girls with the material her mum had brought yesterday. She switched on the wireless and listened to *Housewife's Choice* as she spread the green polka-dot material on the floor. It *was* lovely, she told herself determinedly, not having to worry about being in anyone's way, or about someone treading on a pin as she pinned the paper pattern to the fabric.

Only stopping for a cold fritter and a cup of tea, sweetened with another of the lollipops, Maisie carried on with her dressmaking until the twins' high-pitched voices alerted her to the time. She quickly folded the cut out frocks and put them on top of the treadle before hurrying to the door.

She was amazed to see Dinah and Linda, each holding a hand of a grey-haired lady walking between them as they chattered non-stop. Dilly came up the pathway with a large smile on her face.

"The twins saw the lady walking in front of us, just before we turned into our lane, and they thought it was

Gran. They ran up to her and grabbed her arms, like they do with Gran. Only–"

"When she turned round we saw it wasn't Gran," Linda said, as they reached Maisie.

"We've brought her for a cup of tea because we gave her a shock when we pounced on her," Dinah added.

"I'm Betty Jones, love," the lady said, disentangling her hands and holding her right hand out to Maisie.

"Maisie Butterworth," Maisie replied. "I'm so sorry Linda and Dinah gave you a fright. Come inside and I'll make a pot of tea."

"I'll make it, Mum," Dilly offered. "I'll be careful," she promised.

"My heart did jump a bit," Betty said as she followed Maisie into the living room. "Not so much with fright. Just with... Oh, I don't know. It's just what my own grandkids would have done if they'd still been here. They and my daughter used to live with Tom and me; we're round the corner at number twenty. My daughter lost her first hubby in the war but she remarried a month ago. They live a few miles away now and I miss them something rotten."

"And you and Dilly miss Gran and Grandad and our aunties and uncle and cousins," Linda said. "So we thought we'd bring Mrs Jones for a cup of tea and you could cheer each other up."

"Very persistent, they were," Betty said, as the twins skipped out of the room. "I hope you don't mind, Mrs Butterworth?"

"Not at all. The girls are right. I really miss my mum and everyone. I feel so lonely here. It's lovely to meet a near neighbour. And please call me Maisie." *Because I just know we're going to be friends*, she added silently.

"Betty," Betty said. "I'll organise a coffee morning and introduce you to a few more neighbours, Maisie. I know some will be interested to hear you're good with a sewing machine. Your girls told me you're making them new frocks," she explained. "You know what kids are like for telling life histories."

She smiled as Dilly came in carrying a tray. "Next door but one to me and over the road, too, have got girls about your age, Dilly. You call round at weekend and I'll take you to meet them."

"That would be nice." Dilly said as she put the tray down. "I miss all my cousins but it's Pauline I miss the most because she's ten like me. Shall I bring my lollipop from Gran, Mum? I haven't licked it yet," she added.

Betty roared with laughter. "Seems like you use the kiddies' lollipops to sweeten your tea as well. Gives it a strange taste but better than drinking it sugarless."

*

They were on their second cup of tea when Andy came in. After being introduced to Betty and hearing the tale of how she came to be here, he excused himself to go and start on the garden.

"My Tom would be happy to lend a hand sometime," Betty called after him.

"He works part-time in the park gardens," she said to Maisie. "And he'll be home soon so I best be making a move. I'll fix up that coffee morning very soon, but like I said, I'm at number twenty and you'll be welcome to call any time, especially if you bring Dilly and the twins. Tom would love to meet them."

Maisie was smiling as she saw Betty out. "She does look like your gran from the back," she said to Dilly. "I can understand how Dinah and Linda made the mistake. I'm right glad they did, too."

"So am I, Mum. I can't wait to meet the girls she told me about. I'll wear my new frock if you get it finished in time then their mums might ask you to make them some the same."

"Right now," Maisie said, "I must clear the crockery away and start making us something to eat."

*

Maisie felt happier than she had for ages as she peeled some potatoes. Oh, she'd never stop missing her family but she wouldn't be quite as lonely now she'd made a friend. And Betty knew families with daughters who could be friends for Dilly. Andy and Betty's husband, Tom, might get on well together. That'd be nice.

Betty's going to introduce me to some of her neighbours, too. Maisie's cheerful thoughts continued. If they wanted her to do some dressmaking likely they'd become friends over deciding on material and patterns and taking measurements.

She'd just put the potatoes on to boil when Andy came in with a small bunch of...

"Daffodils," Maisie said. "But where–?"

"Not picked from someone *else's* garden this time, Maisie."

Maisie noticed the little change from Andy's usual assurance. "You mean?"

Andy nodded. "From our own garden, love. Found a whole clump of them when I was clearing away some brambles."

"Oh, Andy. My favourite flowers from my favourite man. It's a perfect end to a perfect day."

"You'll have to call it a daffodil day," Andy said.

Maisie nodded. "And even when the daffodils have stopped flowering, I'll know they're still there in the garden so every day will be a daffodil day."

A Golden Coach

"Look, Janet," said Maurice, "if you don't want to see *High Noon*, I think *An American in Paris* is on at the Palace. We could go there instead."

Janet glanced around the snack bar wishing it wasn't so crowded at lunchtime; she had a feeling this was going to end in an argument. How could she make Maurice understand that she really couldn't go to the pictures with him whatever film it was?

"Maurice, like I said, I've got to keep an eye on Grandad tonight because Mum's going to a meeting and Dad's decorating the Community Centre. It's only a couple of weeks since Grandad had his operation and he won't accept he's got to take things easy. Which is why he can't be left on–"

"Last Saturday you had to take your sister somewhere," Maurice interrupted. "It's always family, family, family with you, Janet."

"It'll be better after the Coronation. It's just there's such a lot of organising to do for the street party." Janet tried to ignore the frown that showed Maurice was becoming exasperated. Maurice thought street parties were for little kids.

"Listen," she said. "You could meet me outside the store when I finish work and come home with me. I'm sure Mum wouldn't mind. We can play records when she's gone to her meeting."

"What about your little sister? Won't you have to look after her?"

Janet shook her head. "Mum's taking Vivian with her."

"So it would be just us two because your grandad will be upstairs in bed?"

"He won't be in bed. I'm going to get him to make some fancy dress costumes out of crêpe paper. Besides," Janet laughed. "Prefabs don't have stairs and Grandad sleeps in the living room on a pull-out bed chair."

"Sorry, Janet. Watching an old man making stuff for a street party while we listen to records isn't my idea of how to spend a Saturday night. Or any night as it happens." Maurice pushed his chair back and stood up. "See you around," he said, before walking off.

*

"And that was that," Janet told her mum later, over a comforting cup of tea at home.

Glad Vivian had gone to call for her best friend and wasn't here to see her big sister upset, Arlene squeezed Janet's shoulder and said, "Maybe it's for the best, love." Secretly, she was relieved it was over before it really started. Janet was a pretty girl with blonde wavy hair and big grey eyes but she'd only just turned sixteen – far too young for a regular boyfriend.

"I know it hurts right now," Arlene continued, "but I don't reckon anyone who can't spare time for family and neighbours could be your Mr Right."

"Well, I've no chance now of finding out if Maurice could have been," Janet said. "Not being able to see him for two Saturdays on a run saw to that. Though tonight's down to him as well. After all, I did invite him round to listen to records. I suppose him being nearly nineteen, he thinks he's too old for that as well as for street parties. I like both so perhaps you're right and it *is* for the best."

Wishing Janet looked as if she really meant that, Arlene said, "There's plenty of lads your age round here enjoying helping get things ready for the party and looking forward to joining in everything."

"Plenty of chaps my age and older and all," Grandad said from his armchair by the fireplace. "I'm as much use as a chocolate fireguard sat here. I should be out and doing along with them. Street parties for coronations have always been something special in our family."

Arlene sighed. She knew her dad was about to go through previous events. Again.

"I met your mum at the party for King Edward, Arlene, our wedding day was the same day George Fifth were crowned and our reception was the street party." He looked from Arlene to Janet, "You were born during the celebrations for King George Sixth's coronation. And I joined in the preparations for each and every party."

"You can join in preparations for this one, too, Grandad," Janet said. "Mrs Butterworth, her who lives on Knott Lane, is sewing costumes for her Dilly and most of the older girls. So I thought while Mum and Vivian are at the meeting, you and me could cut out some fancy dresses for Vivian, her friend Ruth and the Butterworth twins."

"That's a good idea, love." Arlene smiled. She liked seeing Janet's kindness and thoughtfulness towards her grandad who sometimes came across as a grumpy old so-and-so.

"Cutting out paper dresses is a lass's job, Janet," her grandad snapped as if to confirm Arlene's thought.

"Rubbish, Grandad. Who made the queen's dress? *Mr* Norman Hartnell, that's who. He'll have cut out a paper pattern first."

"And, Dad–" Arlene broke off as Vivian burst into the room, followed by Phyllis Clarke, Ruth's mum. "Whatever's wrong?" Arlene asked, noting her daughter's tears.

"Ruth can't come to the street party," Vivian said, gulping. "She's got spots."

"German measles," Phyllis said. "I'm glad she's got them of course, but what a time to do it. I can't stop, Arlene. Ruth's in a right state because she'll have to miss out on everything. Vivian's upset, too, that's why I came back with her. And to tell you I probably won't make tonight's meeting."

Arlene nodded as waves of apprehension whirled through her. She hadn't told anyone except Cliff that she was expecting again. Just three months gone. It could be drastic for her unborn baby if she were to get German measles.

Somehow she managed to say the right things as she saw Phyllis out. Then she went back into the living room where Janet was trying to cheer Vivian up.

"Dad," she demanded, "did I have German measles when I was young?"

"No idea, Arlene."

"I wonder if there's any sort of test the doctor can give me. Ruth was round here yesterday and she'll have been infectious. I need to know if I ever had them."

"We'll have to find out from your mum," her dad said.

Dismayed, Arlene reached for the back of a chair and gripped it tightly. She couldn't cope with this as well. Her mum had passed away seven years ago.

"Don't look so worried, girl. I haven't lost my marbles along with my appendix. I've got my Muriel's big leather notebook in my cupboard. She noted everything in that right from the day we wed."

*

"So there was Dad going through Mum's book," Arlene told Phyllis. Her friend had managed to get to the meeting for the last ten minutes. "And me twitching around like an over-wound clock while he read out dates for when I'd first sat up, crawled, cut my first tooth and so on. It felt like hours 'til he found out I had German measles right badly when I was ten. Honestly, Phyllis, I were that relieved. It isn't a nice thing to have when you're older," she added loudly, nodding slightly towards Vivian skipping along Blakeley Road just ahead of them with the Butterworth twins.

"I'd have broken the news more gently if I'd known," Phyllis said. "But I'd no idea."

Arlene nodded. "Cliff and I weren't going to say anything for a while. And it's still too soon to tell Vivian," she replied quietly. "She'll be thrilled to have a baby brother or sister under the Christmas tree, though, if I'm on time.

"German measles wasn't the only good thing Dad found in Mum's notes, Phyllis. What with Janet due any moment, I couldn't join in hanging flags and banners and suchlike for the last coronation. Instead, I made king and queen and horse puppets and a golden coach out of cut out pictures and sticks for a neighbour's kiddies who had mumps and couldn't be at the street party, either. I'd forgotten all about that 'til Dad read it out."

"And here we are, sixteen years on with the same upset for poor Ruth, only it's German measles."

"Same way of making up a bit for her having to miss out as well," Arlene said. "Dad's busy making puppets and stuff and said to tell you he'll come round to yours on Tuesday and put on a show for Ruth. It'll help him no end and all, Phyllis. He was feeling useless and grumpy with not being able to do much. Now he's like a dog with two tails at the thought of hopefully cheering Ruth up."

"That, along with the promise of her own tray of special coronation food and Betty Jones from number twenty popping in to tell Ruth she can have an extra parcel from the bran tub, should put a bit of a smile back on her face," Phyllis said. "And Daniel, my sister's lad, is sure to come and have a game of Snakes and Ladders with her when he knows. Think the world of each other those two do."

"That's nice," Arlene said, thinking it would have done that Maurice a bit of good to hear how nice folk helped and cared for each other.

"Thank your dad for me," Phyllis said when they reached the Whittakers' prefab. "Tell him I'll make sure there's a bottle of Guinness for the puppet man."

*

"Was it a good meeting, Mum?" Janet asked at breakfast next morning. "We didn't get round to talking about it last night did we?" she added with a grin.

Arlene groaned. "Too many cooks spoiling the broth," she said, remembering what a mess they'd got in all trying to make the golden coach stand upright. "You were the worst, Cliff," she added. "Your way was hopeless."

"Dad's idea was better than Grandad's," said Janet. "And mine was better still."

"But it was me who got it right," Vivian piped up as she poured a mixture of *Bird's Grape Nuts* and *Welgar Shreddies* into her cereal bowl. "It was lucky I came to see what was going on when you were making too much noise for me to sleep."

"You had to use two cereal boxes, though," Janet pointed out. "And now we've got to eat the contents quickly before they go stale."

"That's why I'm having two lots. The meeting was fun, Janet. Some of the dads and big boys are going to paint the kerbs red, white and blue tomorrow. And Mum said she'd make fairy cakes this morning. I'm going to help ice them red, white and blue."

Vivian ate a spoonful of cereal. "Tastes good," she said. "I'll take Grandad some. He can have breakfast in bed. He was tired last night. He kept trying to hide his yawns."

"I hope he stays in bed a while," Arlene whispered. "It'll give me a chance to do the baking in peace."

"If he gets up, I'll ask him if he wants to come to the morning service," said Janet. "I'll even walk him round to the Woodman's Inn if he'll bring me out a lemonade and a packet of crisps."

"Can I come?" Vivian asked. "I like sitting on the tree trunk benches in the children's garden bit."

"Tell you what, chick-a-bid," said Cliff. "When I come back from finishing off at the Community Centre, we'll all go and sit on the Woodman's tree trunk benches and I'll treat us to lemonade and pickled eggs. That's if it doesn't pour with rain again," he added, glancing doubtfully out of the window.

"You can't back out of that offer, Dad," Janet told him. "I'll order an hour of sunshine from one o'clock 'til two."

"Right," said Arlene. "Vivian, you can take your grandad his breakfast. Janet, you clear the table, love. I'll make a start on the baking right away."

Even though they'd been allowed extra sugar and margarine for coronation month, Arlene was as economical as possible with her ingredients. As she weighed and measured carefully, she thought lovingly of Cliff and the surprise he'd sprung on them.

She really hoped the rain would hold off. Going to the Woodman's would help take Vivian's mind off Ruth having to miss out on some of the fun and games, it'd do

Janet good if she was still a bit miserable about that Maurice and Dad would be really chuffed to be going out for a drink. *As for me, I'll be right happy and counting my blessings*, she concluded as she began creaming sugar and margarine.

*

"Can't you make the sun shine like you did on Sunday, Janet?" Vivian asked on Coronation day. It's only raining a bit here but it's pouring down in London, it said so on the wireless."

Janet smiled at her younger sister. "I'll try," she said. "We don't want your special icing to get wet. I still can't believe you used dolly blue for the blue icing, Mum. I thought you could only use that when you're doing the washing. You put it in the rinsing water to make the whites look whiter."

Vivian giggled. "We didn't use much. Only enough to make the icing the right colour."

"Plus it was used for icing four dozen cakes," Arlene added.

"Won't do nobody any harm," her dad said. "I remember how my Muriel used blue ink for the icing on her VE Day cakes."

Arlene guessed her dad was missing her mum a lot today. "So what time are you and Janet going to Ruth's?" she asked to give him something else to think about. Janet had decided to go and help her grandad – saying she'd go to the evening party in the Community Centre.

"About three o'clock. We'll do the puppet show first then Phyllis will bring in the party hats and we'll all have tea together."

"You can help me get Vivian into her fancy dress before you go round to the Clarkes', Janet," said Arlene.

"It won't be easy getting the crown to stay on her mop of hair."

"I don't mind if you cut off some of my curls," Vivian said. "I wish I had blonde wavy hair like you and Mum, Janet."

Janet laughed. "And Mum and I wish we had dark brown curls like you. C'mon, Curly Locks, let's get you into your paper gown."

*

Although it was said you couldn't get German measles more than once, Arlene wasn't taking any chances. But she wanted to see how the puppet show was going and felt sure it would be safe enough if she didn't go inside the Clarkes' prefab.

The party organisers had decided to hold the main events, including the tea, near the Community Centre so everyone could dash inside if it started to rain heavily. After a quick word with some of the other mums, Arlene slipped away and hurried along Blakeley Road towards the Clarkes' at the far end.

They'd been lucky so far, she mused. Drizzly showers with long gaps of cool but dry weather in between. Nothing that had spoilt the Fancy Dress Parade and the games. Hopefully, they'd be able to eat the party tea outdoors. Much more fun for the kiddies that way.

As she walked down the Clarkes' garden path, Arlene smiled when she heard the song that Billy Cotton and his Band and Dickie Valentine, too, had made popular: *In a Golden Coach*. She recognised her dad's gruff voice, Janet's lighter one and young Ruth's slightly squeaky one. But one glorious male voice rose above those and she couldn't wait to see whose it was.

She had to swallow the lump in her throat as she gazed in through the window. Her dad was kneeling behind a long, low table that was covered with grey paper – probably to make it look like a road. The cardboard golden coach, thanks to the stick attached to the back, was moving jerkily along the *road*. Janet, rosy-cheeked and shiny-eyed, was kneeling close to her grandad manipulating the paper people cut outs.

Ruth was sitting on a lad's knee in an armchair opposite the table. Ruth, as she sang, was watching the puppets. The lad with the glorious voice singing about the whole world seeing her beauty, was looking at Janet.

When the song ended, Arlene saw Phyllis wheeling in a wooden trolley piled high with party food. Phyllis obviously noticed Arlene because she said something to Janet and pointed to the window. Janet smiled, jumped up and hurried out of the living room.

A couple of moments later she arrived at Arlene's side. "Ruth loved the puppet show," she said. "Ruth's cousin enjoyed it, too." Arlene hid a smile as her daughter blushed. "He's called Daniel," Janet continued, "and he'll be at the party tonight. And, Mum, he's coming to see Ruth next Sunday, he's going to bring his niece and he wants me and Grandad to put on the puppet show again. He said he'd come to ours afterwards and have a game of chess with Grandad, then listen to records with me. Is that all right?"

Arlene nodded. "Of course it is, love. Now you go in and enjoy the food and company and I'll get back to the others."

*

"So it's been a grand day," Arlene said that night, after relating everything to Cliff as she snuggled close to him in bed. "Vivian didn't miss Ruth too much, Ruth enjoyed herself in spite of having to miss the main party and I reckon her German measles were a blessing in disguise for Dad and our Janet. Daniel seems like a lovely lad. I should think he's already taken Janet's mind off that Maurice."

The Lucky Sixpence

"Hello, Auntie Phyllis," Vivian said. "I've come to play with Ruth."

Phyllis smiled. She wasn't a relation but most of the children round here tended to call their friends' parents Auntie or Uncle, especially if the parents got on well together the way she and Vivian's mum, Arlene, did.

Closer than sisters they were, even though their family life was very different. She was a widow with just Ruth to care for. Arlene had a loving husband and three daughters, the youngest one just over a week old.

"How's your mummy and your baby sister, Vivian?"

"Mummy and Christine are coming home tomorrow. That's why Nana Whittaker's brought me back. Even though it's winter she's spring-cleaning our prefab ready for them. I can't wait to see them. I can't wait to see Ruth, either. Where is she? I really missed her while I was staying at Nana's."

"She's out the back making mud shapes."

Phyllis sighed as Vivian dashed away. Buying *Mr Potato Head* for Ruth's Christmas present had seemed a good idea at first. The plastic pieces, each with a push pin, could be stuck into potatoes and other vegetables to make different funny faced men.

But when Ruth kept asking for a new vegetable because there weren't any firm bits left to stick the pieces into, she'd suggested that Ruth make mud shapes and use them instead of a potato or parsnip. Vegetables weren't fit to be eaten afterwards – not being full of holes. Her war widow's pension wouldn't stretch to food wastage like that. There'd been a lot of extra expense this year what with the Coronation and the trip to the Blackpool illuminations.

Well, last year really. It's 1954 now, Phyllis reminded herself. Only two days until the drama group put on the pantomime. She still didn't know how she'd let herself be talked into playing the part of a chiming clock.

"Mum, can I show Vivian my Christmas presents?" The two little girls bursting in through the back door broke into Phyllis's thoughts.

"Have a good wash first, Ruth."

Ruth giggled and went over to the kitchen sink. "I know I'm all muddy but it was your idea for me to make mud shapes."

When the two friends had disappeared into the living room, Phyllis decided to mix up a batter; she'd leave it to stand while she took Ruth out. It always cooked better after being left a while and she'd use it to make toad in a hole. The sausages were more bread than meat but they'd be tasty enough inside a crisp batter.

The kitchen led into the living room, the girls had left the door open and as she worked Phyllis could hear their excited chatter.

"As well as *Mr Potato Head* I got farm animals, a dolly-dressing book, *Spangles* and some peg dollies," said Ruth.

"Same as I got," Vivian said. "I expect Santa knew we both like the same things."

"And I found this silver sixpence in my Christmas pudding," Ruth continued. "Mummy's taking me to spend it at the toyshop this afternoon. You can come with us if you like."

"I'll have to ask Nana. The toyshop's got some *Pantomime Snap* cards in the window, Ruth. I think they were sevenpence halfpenny, though. But sixpences found in Christmas puddings are lucky ones. You can make a wish on them."

"I didn't know that," said Ruth.

"It's true, Ruth, and you could wish on it to find some pantomime cards that don't cost more than sixpence."

"I love pantomimes," Ruth said. "I'm going to see Cinderella at the Community Centre. Mummy's in it."

"I'd like to see it," said Vivian. "I might be busy helping with my baby sister, though. I know Santa didn't really bring her but she was my very best Christmas present."

"Santa didn't bring me the thing I wanted most in the whole world," Ruth said. "I didn't think he would. Not really."

"Don't wish on your lucky sixpence for pantomime cards then. Wish for what you want the most. And you can tell me what it is because I'm your best friend."

Phyllis moved closer to the door wondering what it was her daughter wanted so much.

"My daddy died before I was even born," said Ruth. "So my wish is that there was someone else who'd be my daddy."

Oh, sweetheart, I wish there were, too, Phyllis thought. Her Jack had been killed during the last weeks of the war. He hadn't even known she was pregnant.

Phyllis often felt lonely and Jack wouldn't have wanted her to be on her own for ever. But she hadn't found anyone she could build a relationship with. Not recently, anyway. She hadn't actually met many single men of the right age at all. That was one reason she'd joined the drama group, she'd hoped she might meet someone there.

Sighing, she went to the cooker, lit the gas and put the kettle on. It had just started to whistle merrily when Vivian's grandma came for Vivian. "Stay and have a cup of tea," suggested Phyllis. It would be good to have someone to talk to instead of brooding.

"You're not making it with them new-fangled tea bag things, are you? The paper round the tea leaves gives the tea a right funny taste."

"No. It's proper tea made in a teapot," Phyllis replied.

"Just a quick cup, then. I've still a bit to get done ready for Arlene and baby Christine coming home tomorrow."

"I'm looking forward to seeing Christine," said Phyllis.

Mrs Whittaker smiled. "Arlene told me she'd asked you to be godmother. Her sister, Josie, will be the other one and her middle brother's going to be godfather."

"You mean Ralph? Is he coming all the way from Malta?" Phyllis knew he'd settled there after the war. She'd met him a couple of years ago when he'd come to visit Arlene and had liked him a lot. She remembered wishing there was time for them to get to know each other better but he'd only stayed a week before going back.

"He doesn't live there any more." Mrs Whittaker held her cup out for a refill. "He came home for good at Christmas. He's stopping at mine 'til he can find a place of his own. Got himself a job already. Starts next week."

"It'll be good to see him again," said Phyllis, deciding she'd ask Maisie Butterworth who lived on Knott Lane to run her up something pretty to wear for the christening. Right good at making dresses Maisie were.

Mrs Whittaker nodded and called to Vivian. "Sitting here won't buy the baby a new bonnet," she said.

"If you let me go to the toyshop with Ruth this afternoon, there's a place two doors down that sells baby clothes," said Vivian. "They might have a bonnet for Christine."

Her gran laughed. "It's just a saying, lass. Means sitting here won't get the work done."

"But can Vivian come to the toyshop, please?" asked Ruth.

"If your mum agrees," Mrs Whittaker replied.

Phyllis smiled at the two girls and told Vivian to come back at two o'clock so they could catch the two-twenty bus from the stop on the main road.

*

"Auntie Phyllis, do you remember my uncle Ralph?" Vivian asked when she returned at two o'clock with a tall, dark-haired man.

Phyllis nodded and felt warmth flood her face. She'd thought of Ralph while eating her lunchtime soup but she hadn't expected to see him so soon. He was even more attractive than she'd remembered.

"Nana left her rheumatics medicine behind," Vivian explained. "So he brought it for her. He wants to come to the toy shop and buy a teddy bear for Christine."

Phyllis nodded again, wishing she hadn't become tongue-tied.

"It's good to see you again, Phyllis." Ralph's brown eyes held a hint of amusement and, Phyllis thought hopefully as they shook hands, maybe a hint of admiration, too. "I hope you won't mind company?" he added with a smile.

"Not at all," she replied, praying she hadn't sounded as breathless as she felt. She turned away and grabbed her shopping bag off the table. "We'd best get a move on if we want to catch the bus."

Vivian and Ruth ran ahead chattering excitedly. Ralph fell easily into step with Phyllis and, for a while, they walked in silence.

"It's grand to be home," he began, just as Phyllis said, "Are you glad to be home?"

They laughed. "That's my question answered," said Phyllis.

He nodded. "It's even better to meet up again with people I like, knowing there's time to build friendships now."

"Your mother said you're looking for somewhere to live. Are you hoping to find something in this area?"

"I'd like to be near Arlene and Cliff and my nieces. So far, I've missed out on being a proper uncle to Janet and Vivian because of the war and staying on in Malta. I want to get to know them better. It will be easier with Christine of course. I'll know her from babyhood. I'll be taking my responsibilities of being her godfather quite seriously."

The two of them discussed becoming godparents until they reached the bus stop. Then Ralph joined in Vivian and Ruth's chatter. When they got on the bus, he squeezed in on the same seat as them.

It's clear he adores kids, Phyllis thought as she watched and listened. He's so nice and I hope Ruth and I are two of the people he wants to build a friendship with. I've a feeling that could lead to something really special.

There was a sale on at the toyshop. Ruth was delighted to find a pack of *Pantomime Snap* cards marked down to sixpence. "There's a picture of Cinderella and a clock on the front, Mummy." Ruth looked up at Ralph. "Cinderella's going to be on at the Community Centre." She giggled. "And Mummy's the clock."

"That's nice. It means she'll always know the right time for things to happen," Ralph said. He smiled across at Phyllis and her heart fluttered.

"I'll pay for the cards, Ruth," Phyllis said quickly. "You keep your lucky sixpence, poppet." Then the wish you made on it might come true, she added silently.

There was a pack of *Happy Families* in the sale, too. Ralph bought that for Vivian then they all had fun choosing a teddy bear for Christine.

"What about Janet?" Ralph asked Vivian. "Your big sister's too old for toys."

"She likes jigsaws." Vivian pointed to some and Ralph bought one with five hundred pieces.

"Can Vivian and her uncle come for tea and then we can all play cards afterwards?" Ruth asked as they left the shop. "We're having toad in the hole," she told Ralph.

"There won't be many toads, Ralph," Phyllis said, laughing. "I've only two sausages to make them with. But you're welcome to share them."

"We could call in at the chippy for a take-out on the way home," Ralph suggested. "We'll get everything double-wrapped so they'll still be hot when we get home. My treat," he added looking at Phyllis.

"We can get some fish and chips for Nana, and Janet will be home from work," Vivian said. "Daddy's going to see Mummy and Christine so he won't want any."

"Your mother won't want Arlene's smelling of fish and chips after she's spent all day cleaning and polishing," Phyllis said to Ralph. "She and Janet had better come to mine as well."

*

It's so cosy and homely, Phyllis thought contentedly as she glanced round the living room after they'd eaten. Swirl patterned curtains closed against the dark, coal fire glowing and the dark wood, gate leg table fully extended so they could all sit round it to play Happy Families.

"It's nice for the children to have a mummy *and* a daddy," Ruth said. She showed everyone her Mr Dough the Baker, Mrs, Miss and Master Dough cards before placing the family face down on the table. "I wonder if the wish I made on my lucky sixpence will come true."

"She wished for a daddy," Vivian piped up. "You could be her daddy, Uncle Ralph. Ruth likes you a lot, she told me, didn't you, Ruth?"

Ruth nodded. "I think Mummy likes him, too, because she's laughed a lot since he came."

"I'll go and make a pot of tea." Aware her cheeks were flaming Phyllis jumped up and hurried into the kitchen.

Her face had only just cooled down when Ralph came through from the living room. "We haven't known each other long, Phyllis," he said. "But I enjoyed being with you during that week I spent at Arlene's a couple of years ago and I often thought about you after I went back to Malta. I've enjoyed today as well and I think you have, too?"

Tongue-tied again, Phyllis nodded.

So how about we see a lot more of each other, you, me and Ruth? And, who knows, maybe a wish made on a lucky sixpence might come true. Before I came to join you, I got a Happy Family," he added. "Mr Clock the clockmaker, his wife Mrs Clock and their children. Seeing as you're a clock in the pantomime, I think that could be a good omen for us."

Phyllis smiled up at him. It wasn't that she was tongue-tied this time – more that words didn't seem necessary.

Lonely Valentine

"Whoever it was said February can be the cruellest month got it right," said Anita, shivering as she walked into the kitchen.

Her mum nodded. "It's the coldest one I've known since we came to live here. And I haven't got the living room fire going yet. Not that it would make much difference. That's the downside of prefabs, they're almost impossible to keep warm in this weather. Tell you what, love," she added, "I'll light the gas oven and leave the door open and we'll eat in here. I've made porridge."

Anita pulled the ironing board down from the wall so they could use it as a table then, smiling, went to get a couple of chairs. It was a good job her dad wasn't home from working his night shift yet, he wouldn't approve of eating off the ironing board, or of using the gas oven to keep them warm. Bit of a stickler for things like that, was Dad.

"This is probably the only chance I'll have of eating anything until this evening," Anita said as she sprinkled sugar on her porridge. "It will be extra busy at work today with everyone wanting a shampoo and set so they look good for the Valentine's dances."

"I hope you're going to one as well?"

Anita shook her head and concentrated on eating. With Michael away doing his National Service dressing up and making herself look attractive to go somewhere she'd be mixing with other lads would feel like she was being disloyal to him. But she'd explained this many times before; she didn't want to get involved in that sort of conversation again.

Her mum obviously had no such qualms, though, because she sighed loudly before saying, "Doesn't seem right staying home on a Saturday night at your age."

"It wouldn't *seem right* going to a Valentine's dance without Michael, either, Mum. Besides, I won't exactly be staying at home; I'm baby-sitting for Richard and Josie so they can go to the Community Centre."

"That's no different really. You'll still be stuck indoors on your own instead of out enjoying yourself with others."

Anita smiled. Josie had been one of her first customers at the hairdressing salon; they'd got on well and had soon become good friends. Richard was nice, too, and Anita enjoyed going round to their place.

"They've got a television you know, Mum. So I'll be doing something a lot of others round here can't do and that's watching *Saturday Night at the London Palladium*," she said, getting to take her empty pots to the sink.

And hopefully, she added silently, I'll have a Valentine's card from Michael and maybe a letter as well to keep me company.

It wouldn't be long before she knew. She almost always saw Robert the postman on her way to the bus stop.

*

As she opened the garden gate, Anita stopped a moment to glance at the snowdrops which, in spite of the frozen earth, were making a brave show beneath the leafless lilac tree. This was the third year they'd bloomed. The first time had been on Wednesday February 13th 1952 – almost two years ago to the day – there'd only been two tiny snowdrops then.

Anita remembered it clearly; it was the day before Michael had left. He'd kissed her goodbye at the gate and, afterwards, she'd pointed to the flowers and quoted lines from a poem written by the Victorian poet, Annie Matheson: *Two little snowdrops, in green and white, Came out of the darkness and into the light, and softly kissed one another.*

Remembering that kiss was bittersweet. It had been so special, yet it also made her miss Michael all the more. But it wouldn't be too long now before he came back.

She could see Robert up ahead now and, trying not to slip on the icy pavement, she quickened her step. She felt sure he'd have something for her. He was Michael's brother and for her twenty-first birthday last year, and for Valentine's Day as well, Michael had posted cards for her to Robert way ahead of time and asked Robert to deliver them on the right day.

Robert looked grim as he stood waiting for her. Probably frozen to the marrow, she thought. She greeted him jokingly, "Nice weather if you're a polar bear."

His face didn't crack when he handed her an envelope. "It's a card," he said. "But it isn't from our Michael. Not his writing and anyway it was posted local."

"You've got a card or letter for me from Michael, though? One he posted to you early on so you could–"

She broke off as Robert shook his head. Looked closely at him trying to see if he was having her on. He had to be, didn't he?

"Oh, I get it," she said. "It isn't actually Valentine's Day 'til tomorrow. I just thought with it falling on a Sunday you'd be bringing it today but you're coming round with it tomorrow, is that it?"

"Sorry, Anita. Michael hasn't sent me anything to deliver to you. You've got a card from somebody, though, haven't you? Sealed with a loving kiss as well." He jabbed a gloved hand at the card he'd given her which had the letters S.W.A.L.K. on the envelope.

Anita frowned and ripped the envelope open. Pulled out a card – all satin and cobwebby lace. Looked inside. "It's from "A Secret Admirer"," she said.

"Oh, I recognise this hand writing, it's my boss's son's. He's only eighteen and he knows I'm spoken for. At least, I think I am... I hope I am," she added wistfully. Oh, heck, she was so disappointed there was no card from Michael, she'd be crying if she said any more.

Perhaps Robert guessed that because he touched her arm lightly and said, "Michael could've sent something to me to give you and it's got delayed. It might arrive Monday and I'll bring it Tuesday. Or he might even have posted it direct to you. Whatever he's done, it'll be better getting it a day or two late than not at all, won't it?"

Robert's words didn't bring her much comfort as she walked towards the bus stop. She hadn't heard from Michael since Christmas. He wasn't good at writing regularly but there wasn't usually a six week gap between letters. And when he did write, well, his letters were friendly but not exactly romantic. She worried sometimes that he wasn't as serious about her as she was about him.

*

"What's up, Anita? You look like a cat what's just lost a kipper. You haven't gone and cut me hair wrong, have you?"

Anita smiled at her last customer of the day and shook her head. "Your hair is going to look lovely,

Maureen. The poodle cut will really suit you. But I feel like someone's blown my ankles up with a bicycle pump. I've been on my feet for over eight hours without a sit down."

"You'll have to stick them in warm water and mustard when you get home else you'll not be fit for going dancing tonight. Where are you going? The Valentine's Dance at the Salford Palais is always good."

"I'm baby-sitting for friends so they can go dancing," Anita said. "They've got a television set so I'll be watching a variety show or a play." Gosh, she'd said that so many times today she must sound like a record that had got stuck.

"Your boyfriend keeping you company, is he?" Maureen asked with a cheeky smile.

"Michael's still doing his National Service. Last time he wrote he said he'd be home before Easter so it won't be that long before I see him again."

"I'm glad my Roy did his when he did. Went in just before they put it up to two years."

"I wish Michael had gone in before they did that but he waited 'til he'd finished his plumbing apprenticeship."

"Eighteen months was bad enough," said Maureen. "It's a long time to spend away from each other. I couldn't stop wondering if he'd still want to be my boyfriend when he came out. I mean you do worry about things like that, don't you?"

Anita sighed and nodded.

"Feelings can change when you're not together," Maureen continued. "Especially the fella's with all the socialising when they've got a twenty four hour pass but it's not long enough to get home."

Anita wasn't sure if Maureen was making her feel better or worse. Because, of course, she sometimes thought the same things about herself and Michael.

"Awful at writing, Roy was," said Maureen. "Managed to send me a couple of lovely Valentine's cards, though. I know you aren't supposed to, but he put his name on them, bless him. And everything turned out all right for me and Roy in the end. Did you get a Valentine's card from your Michael, Anita?"

Anita quickly reached for the hand mirror to show Maureen the back of her hair. As she'd hoped, Maureen was so busy admiring her new hairstyle that she didn't say another word about boyfriends or Valentine's cards. But, silly or not, Anita decided there and then she'd take last year's Valentine's card from Michael with her tonight to dream over while she was baby-sitting.

*

"Was the baby good for you, Anita?" her mum asked at breakfast the next morning.

Dad was at home today so they were eating at the proper table. He must have got up early and lit the fire, Anita thought. It was burning away merrily and, although there'd been ice on the inside of the bedroom and bathroom windows, it felt quite warm here in the living room.

"She was as good as gold, Mum. I gave her a bottle at ten o'clock, had a lovely cuddling time afterwards and she went straight to sleep when I put her back in her cot."

"Did you enjoy the television programmes, Anita?" asked her dad.

Anita hid a smile when she felt her mum kicking her lightly under the table. She knew Mum wanted her to answer enthusiastically. Mum had been trying to persuade Dad to get a television set for months. "Oh, I did, Dad," Anita replied. "*Saturday Night at the Palladium* had some lovely performers on and then there was a Scotland Yard case history. That was really good."

"Did Josie and Richard enjoy the dance?" asked her mum, clearly pretending she wasn't interested in what had been on the television.

"They did. But I think they're home-birds really, Mum. Just happy being together in their lovely little house."

Anita loved her job as a hairdresser but she always felt a bit jealous when she saw Richard and Josie's contentment. It was what she dreamed of for her and Michael one day. That's if... Maureen's words from yesterday kept playing in her head: "Feelings can change when you're not together." That's what she'd said. And seeing how Michael hadn't written for weeks and it seemed, too, like he hadn't sent her a Valentine's card, maybe his feelings had changed.

"I don't want another cuppa thanks, Mum. I think I'll go and read my *Hairdressers Journal*. Got to keep up with all the latest hairstyles and products."

Once in her bedroom, Anita lay on her bed, under the eiderdown, and continued to brood. It wasn't like her to feel like this. Oh, she missed Michael all the time but she usually thought happy thoughts of how it would be when he came home. That's what she should be doing now, she told herself crossly. So, do it.

She hadn't meant to fall asleep but realised she must have done when she became aware of a voice from the wireless in the living room: "The time in Britain is twelve noon, in Germany it's one o'clock, but home and away it's time for Two-Way Family Favourites."

It was a ritual for the three of them to listen to the programme together before Dad went down to the

Woodman's Inn for a quick half before Sunday dinner. Anita jumped off the bed and arrived in the living room just as the signature tune was ending.

Seeing Mum and Dad sitting in their armchairs either side of the fire, Mum's knitting needles clicking quietly and the aroma of *Erinmore* from Dad's pipe, brought the yearning feeling back again. Would her dreams for her and Michael ever come true?

Anita settled down on the sofa only half-listening to the messages to and from loved ones and the songs or piece of music they'd requested. It came as somewhat of a shock to suddenly hear her own name and a song request for her from Michael. She was aware of Mum letting her knitting drop into her lap and Dad putting his pipe on the hearth and turning the wireless up as Bing Crosby sang *May I*? especially for her.

"It's a proposal, Anita," her mum said. "Michael's got Bing to say what he himself feels for you. He adores you, wants to hear you say *I do*. Oh, Anita, isn't it so romantic?"

"I... I..." Anita couldn't say any more; she just let her tears flow.

"Silly goose," her dad said gruffly as he got up from his chair and stepped over to her holding out a white handkerchief.

Smiling, Anita mopped her tears before passing the handkerchief over to her mum.

*

"This was the best Sunday dinner ever," Anita said later. Her dad had brought a large bottle of lemonade home from the Woodman's and made them all a Martini and lemonade to drink with their meal because it was a special occasion.

"It's a shame we've got to do something as mundane as washing the pots," her mum said, laughing.

Anita collected the used plates together and stood, ready to take them through to the kitchen. Before she had time to move there was a rapping at the front door. "I'll go," she said. "It'll be another neighbour come to ask me if I heard my name on the wireless. Half of Broome Park village must have called today."

"And the other half asked me the same thing in the Woodman's," said her dad.

Smiling, Anita walked into the hall. When she opened the door she gasped and blinked. That martini Dad had made must have been stronger than she'd realised.

"Anita?" He sounded shy and uncertain. "Did you hear it? Did you hear–?"

"Michael. I can't believe it's really you. Oh, Michael." Half-crying, half-laughing, she moved towards him and sighed happily as his arms went round her and pulled her close.

"When did you get home?"

"About two hours ago. I said a quick as possible hello to Mum and Dad and then came to see if–"

"Did Robert know you'd be here for Valentine's Day?"

"He knew I'd be here either today or tomorrow. He said he felt awful that he couldn't even drop you a hint, Anita. But I'd sworn him to secrecy."

Anita sniffed against his shoulder. "I was upset not to get a card from you," she said.

"Oh, Anita," he murmured into her ear, "I wanted to bring myself instead of sending a card. I could never seem to write the words to tell you how much I was missing you, how much I loved you. That's why I didn't write very often. But I loved you more every day even though we were apart. I just hope you...?"

He moved back slightly and gazed down at her.

If the message on the wireless hadn't already done so, Michael's words and the anxious look in his gorgeous brown eyes would have cast away any doubts Anita had ever had about his feelings for her.

"I was sometimes a bit worried about why you didn't mention loving me in your letters," she admitted. "But when I heard the message on the wireless–"

"I wrote in to the programme a few weeks ago when I hadn't got an actual date for my demob and wasn't sure I'd get here on time," he said. "I knew you and your folks always listen to it. That song of Bing's was the only way I could think of to let you know how I feel."

"It was lovely," said Anita. "Really romantic."

Michael smiled as he twisted round some of the words from the song. "Tell me my fate, sweetheart. What is your answer? Are you going to say *I do*?"

"Come to the gate and I'll answer you there," she whispered.

*

As they stood by the gate, entwined in love, Anita pointed to the snowdrops.

"Remember the day you went away, Michael? I said a line from a poem? *Two little snowdrops in green and white rose out of the darkness and into the light, and softly kissed one another*. Well, just like our love, the snowdrops have kept blooming. There's more of them now, of course, and I'm not sure if I could love you any more than I do already. I love you with all my heart, Michael, and my answer is yes.

"Yes please," she added breathlessly a few minutes later.

Then they both laughed as they turned to see Anita's mum and dad standing arm in arm at the door and heard them singing *May I*?

A Silver Lining

It was the same bus conductor as the last few days. He smiled when he came to collect Maisie's fare. "Hospital stop is it? You'll brighten up the patients' day in that pretty frock."

Maisie forced herself to smile back. He always seemed to find something nice to say. Tries to cheer all his passengers up, she realised, as he walked down the bus whistling *Look for the Silver Lining.*

Well, all right, she'd look. It was summer so heating bills would be less, her neighbours sometimes gave her fruit and salad stuff from their gardens because she and Andy were still working on clearing and digging over what would be their garden. And, in the few months they'd been living in the prefab village, she'd managed to earn a little from her dressmaking. She mustn't forget Betty Jones, neither. Turned out to be a right good friend, Betty had. Dilly and the twins loved her, too, she were like an extra auntie to them.

But the good things didn't really outweigh the not so good. If Andy had to go and get a broken leg, why did he have to get it falling off the prefab roof? An accident at work would have meant injury benefit money instead of just sickness pay. Twelve and six a week for the rent seemed an enormous amount to find out of that measly amount. Bus fares mounted up as well. But she couldn't not visit Andy every day.

Oh, heck, they were at the hospital now – Andy mustn't guess she was worried; she'd better get her bright face back on. Not easy when he'd be propped up in the bed with that traction thing on his poor broken leg.

*

Maisie's breath caught in her throat and she felt her heart pounding as she stood at the end of Andy's empty bed.

"It's all right, Maisie." The patient in the next bed reassured her quickly. "He's gone to have a bit of his plaster snipped off. 'Twas rubbing him and he got a sore spot."

"Thanks, Duggie. I did get a bit of a fright." Maisie smiled at the young man. He and her Andy had become friendly what with being side by side and they often chatted to each other's visitors. "How's the arm?"

"Not up to strong-arm tactics yet," he said. "You're looking as pretty as a picture today if you don't mind me saying. Is that dress one of your own creations?"

Maisie nodded.

"Andy was telling me how good you are at dressmaking. Said you made all the kiddies' clothes, too. And dresses and suchlike for other people."

"I like doing it," Maisie said. "I'd feel lost without my sewing."

"Don't suppose you fancy selling on a market? My family and I have got stalls on Radlington Market but Mum's not been so well lately. She's looking for someone to take hers on. She sells hats she makes herself. Standing on the market's got a bit much for her, though. She needs someone to do the selling and she's always wanted to sell frocks, skirts and blouses alongside her hats. I mentioned it to Andy last night." Duggie grinned, "But here's the fella himself. You and he should have a chinwag about you running Mum's stall."

*

Maisie waited impatiently while the nurses settled Andy back in bed. She missed him so much; she couldn't wait for a kiss and cuddle. But at last the nurses bustled away.

"So," Andy said, after the greeting Maisie had been waiting for. "Is Betty minding the girls and how are they today?"

"Yes, they're round at Betty and Tom's. Dilly and Linda are fine, missing you of course. Dinah's fine, too, really. Just quieter than usual. I reckon she thinks you being in here is her fault seeing as you climbed on the roof to get her doll down. She's upset about her dolly's legs as well. They smashed when you fell. I offered to make Amelia Jane some but Dinah said legs made from stuffed material wouldn't be the same."

"Talking of you making things, Maisie..."

Maisie shuffled her chair closer to the bed and spoke more quietly. "You mean like me selling the dresses and things I make on a market stall? Duggie were talking about that while I was waiting for you. Said he'd mentioned it to you. What do you reckon to it?"

"I'm likely to be off work a good few weeks so extra money would come in handy. It'd be putting a lot onto your shoulders though, Maisie. The market's on three days a week and then there'd be all the extra dressmaking you'd have to do. But I'd be able to look after the girls when they come home from school and Dilly's a good lass, she'd help me make the tea and do a bit of tidying."

"You wouldn't mind doing that?"

"'Course I wouldn't. Not that much difference pushing the *Ewbank* over the floor than pushing trolleys around the station and keeping things clean and tidy."

The idea began to take hold in her mind now. It would be nice not having to worry so much about how they'd pay the bills. She could get to the market by train – travel for free because of Andy working for British Rail. Take her stock in suitcases. Just think what it would be like seeing dresses she'd made hanging up on a rail with price tickets on and lots of potential customers looking at them.

"Let's talk it over a bit more with Duggie," Maisie said.

*

"If you took the stall on," Duggie told her, "Mum would want all the profit on any of her hats you sell. That means she'd still be earning the same for doing less work so she'd be more than willing to keep paying the rent money for the stall."

"Really?" said Maisie.

"Only fair that is," Duggie replied. "You wouldn't have to worry about getting to the market at the crack of dawn, neither. My brother Sid, who runs the pot stall with me, would see to the setting up of Mum's stall, putting the hats out and rails up for your dresses."

"So what do you think, Maisie?" Andy looked more cheerful than Maisie had seen him look since his accident. "Do you fancy being the Norman Hartnell of Radlington market?"

"I reckon I might," she replied.

The three of them continued to chat and discuss things and Maisie could tell both Andy and Duggie were as disappointed as she was when the end of visiting bell rang.

*

"Well, that's right good news, love," Betty said when Maisie told her about the market stall. "When are you going to start?"

"In a few weeks. I'll have to wait 'til Andy's home and managing on his crutches." Maisie glanced towards her daughters who were playing Piggy-in-the-Middle. "The girls will be back at school by then, so giving an eye to them won't be too much for him."

"If you started sooner, would you have anything of yours ready to sell?"

"I could have because I was thinking on the bus on the way home that I'd have a rail of kiddies' clothes as well. They don't take as long to make. I've quite a few things made that I use to show folk when they're thinking of getting me to make something for them."

"So, you could be up and running in, say, a couple of weeks?"

"But for the girls I could. I doubt Andy will be home that quick."

"How about you find someone to look after the girls? Someone who lives round the corner from you who loves kiddies and misses her grandchildren something rotten."

"Betty. You wouldn't? What about Tom, wouldn't he mind?"

"He'd be made up, Maisie. So what do you say?"

Thoughts and plans whirred through Maisie's head. She'd have to go and have a look round the market, try and work out what sort of clothes future customers would like. She'd fix up a meeting with Duggie's brother for this coming Wednesday. Oh, heck, this was so scary everything about to happen sooner than expected. Because, of course, she'd take up Betty's offer. But only if...

"I'll pay you for minding the girls, Betty. It'll help you save up enough to have those few days away in October you said you'd like now your Tom's retired. I won't do it otherwise," she said as Betty looked as if she were about to protest. "I'll be needing someone at times when Andy goes back to work, too. I hadn't really thought that far ahead."

Betty smiled. "I was about to say my offer was for the future as well."

"Let's call the girls over and tell them about it," said Maisie.

"Is it because Daddy's leg will never get mended like Amelia Jane's legs won't?" Dinah asked in a wavery voice when Maisie had explained things.

Maisie immediately felt guilty. How hadn't she guessed what her little daughter was thinking? "Oh, sweetheart," she said, hugging her close. "Daddy's leg *will* get mended, really it will. It's just going to take a little while."

"And then he'll go back to work?"

Maisie nodded. "He'll soon be pushing loaded trolleys around his station again."

"That's all right then, isn't it Dinah?" said Linda.

Dinah looked at her twin and nodded.

"And I hope you'll still have the market stall when I'm old enough to come and work with you, Mum," Dilly said. "That'd be all right as well."

*

"Is it always this busy, Sid?" Maisie asked as they made their way to talk to yet another stall-holder. She was enjoying the noise, the smells and the bustle and felt quite over-awed by the friendliness of the market folk she'd already met.

"A hot day brings customers," Sid replied. "But I don't reckon you'll ever go short of them, Maisie. Our mam's stall is always busy, your dresses and clothes will sell like hot cakes along with the hats."

Both Sid and Duggie talk in clichés half the time, thought Maisie, hiding a grin. Must be something to do with working on the market.

Sid hooked his hand through the crook of Maisie's arm. "This stall–" he began. But Maisie interrupted.

"That little shop over there, Sid. It's a dolls' hospital."

Sid nodded. "There's almost nothing Jonty Myers can't do with a broken toy. It's a right Aladdin's cave in there. They've trays of dolls' eyes and limbs and all sorts. You thinking of asking if they'd like you to supply them with dolls' clothes? Could be a good idea, that."

Maisie explained about Dinah's broken doll. "If Jonty could give it some new legs, Dinah might believe Andy's leg will mend as good as new as well."

*

"So, that was my day, Betty. After meeting other stall-holders I don't feel quite as nervous about things. 'Course, I'll need to burn the candle both ends making enough to sell." Maisie laughed. "I must have caught the habit of talking in clichés already," she said, and went on to tell Betty how Sid and Duggie used them all the time.

"But the best part really, was seeing the dolls' hospital. Jonty, the doll doctor, said it'll be no problem to give Dinah's dolly new legs. He gave me a little appointment card with Amelia Jane's name on. Dinah's not let it out of her sight. The appointment's tomorrow. So, do you fancy a morning out, Betty? Come with us and, even though the market's not on, I can show you the spot I'll be selling from."

"That would be grand, Maisie. You know, I thank my lucky stars for the day you Butterworths came to live in our prefab village."

"Gosh, Betty." Maisie laughed again. "You're talking clichés now as well."

"To clichés," said Betty, raising her glass of lemonade.

"And to good neighbours and silver linings," Maisie added. "The silver lining in Andy's accident is going to be me selling my Daffy-down Dilly clothes for ladies and children on Radlington Market."

All's Well That Ends Well

"Mummy, Mummy, Mummy!"

The twins' urgent cries came from the garden. Maisie frowned and quickly unplugged the iron before hurrying to the back door.

Dinah and Linda were running up the long path between the flowerbeds of snapdragons, marigolds and cornflowers. Maisie breathed a sigh of relief; it was obvious neither of the sometimes accident-prone eight-year-olds were hurt.

"Gloria needs some sharp scissors," Linda shrieked.

"She's found a little dog stuck in the brambles in the bit of park on the other side of our fence," panted Dinah as the two of them reached Maisie.

"Daddy's secateurs will be better than scissors to cut brambles," said Maisie.

"No." Linda shook her head. "Gloria said she'll have to cut his hair from the brambles 'cos it's long hair and it's got all twisted round in the thorny bits."

As she hurried to fetch her dress-making scissors Maisie wondered what the lass from next door had been doing in that part of the park. The stretch behind the prefabs' back gardens was wasteland really – not tended to like the rest. The little ones often played there, but Gloria was eighteen. Surely she wouldn't have been doing a bit of courting – not at this time of day.

"Oh, well, I'll find out soon enough," she murmured as she joined her impatient daughters.

"See," said Linda, pointing, when they got closer to the fence, "there's Gloria's head bobbing around."

"Gloria must be kneeling over the poor dog," said Dinah. "C'mon. Run faster, Mummy."

*

"Am I glad to see you, Mrs Butterworth," said Gloria, holding up a hand for the scissors as Maisie climbed over the fence. "This poor little fella's in a right state. Could you hold each bit of bramble while I snip the hair? And perhaps Dinah and Linda could stroke his head and talk gentle to him. He won't bite; he knows we're helping him."

"I wonder what his name is?" whispered Dinah.

"He's not wearing a collar," said Gloria. "Could have come off somewhere I suppose. Flipping heck. I'll have to cut right close to his skin to get him free of this bit of branch."

"Let's call him Patch," Linda suggested, kneeling next to her twin. "He's got black and brown patches and Gloria found him in this bramble patch."

"Don't be frightened, Patch," said Dinah. "Gloria and Mummy won't be long and then you'll be able to get up."

But when Gloria had finished snipping it was clear the little dog hadn't the strength to move. "Could we take him into yours, Mrs Butterworth?" Gloria asked, gently picking him up. "Only I don't think our cat would take too kindly to having him around. She's nasty when it comes to dogs."

"You were ironing weren't you, Mummy?" said Linda, as they walked up the garden. "If we empty the un-ironed clothes out of the basket and put a cushion in, it would make a comfy bed for Patch."

Maisie nodded. "You two run ahead and get his bed ready then. And fill a small dish with water and sprinkle a bit of sugar in. A sweet drink might do him good."

"It's a shame our Dilly's staying at Gran's," said Dinah. "She'll be cross she's missed this."

"The twins will enjoy being one up on their big sister," Gloria said with a smile as they ran off.

*

"He looks a little bit brighter now," said Gloria gazing down at Patch a little while later. "Apart from his raggedy haircut," she added with a sigh. "Still, it'll grow back again. And I think I managed to get all those nasty thorns out of his poor side."

"He doesn't want any more to drink," Linda said.

"Put a blanket over him and just let him rest in the basket," said Gloria.

"Are you a vet or a nurse, Gloria?" Dinah asked.

"No. I worked in Woolies before we moved here. But I love animals."

"Were you looking for mice or squirrels in the park? Is that what you were doing there?"

Gloria laughed. "It's such a lovely day I decided to walk home through the park. I'd been helping out up at Broome Hall," she added. "Dad's her ladyship's chauffer and he offered my services. Everywhere is a right mess after–" She broke off and glanced at Maisie.

Maisie knew Gloria was referring to the burglary that had taken place last week. "Tell you what," she said to the twins. "I saw Policeman Ken earlier, when I went to the grocery van. He's got a day off. You run across and tell him we've found a small, long-haired terrier. Someone might have reported him missing at the police station."

The girls ran off happily. They liked the local bobby who lived on Blakeley Road in what everyone called the *Police Prefab*.

"Is there any news about the burglary, Gloria?" Maisie asked. "I'm glad the Hall's at the far side of the park. Wouldn't like to think of a burglar being close to us. Though I shouldn't think anyone living in the prefabs has anything worth stealing."

"Most of the stolen goods were found the day after the burglary in the old air raid shelter in the Hall's gardens," said Gloria. "They reckon the burglar hid them there meaning to go back for them some time. But the jewellery wasn't there. A diamond bar brooch and matching stud earrings. The thief probably put *them* in his pocket. I hope the brooch pin sticks in him where it'll hurt the most. Her ladyship's right upset at losing them; they were a present from her son who was killed in the war."

"Let's hope the police manage to catch the burglar," said Maisie. "I suppose they'll be keeping a watch on the air raid shelter hoping he'll return."

"I think so. A lot of the doors inside the Hall were damaged. Wouldn't surprise me if the workmen fitting new ones aren't police, they're taking long enough over the job."

A small woof from the laundry basket prevented any more talk of the burglary as Gloria reached for the dish of water and watched Patch lap eagerly. "He's making a quick recovery. How can we find out who he belongs to if nobody's reported him missing? I'll ask the staff up at the Hall if they've heard of anyone who's lost a terrier dog. They might of because they often walk round the park when they're off-duty. But what are we going to do with him meantime?"

"He can stay here," said Maisie. "I'm sure his owner will be in touch with the police and Ken will let other police stations know we've got him. And my Andy often calls in at the Woodman's for a quick half after work. I'll ask him to mention it there. I doubt it will be long before his owner turns up. I'll have to make sure the twins understand that, else they'll get too fond of him."

*

Three days went by before a man and woman called at Maisie's saying she might have their dog. For some reason, Maisie didn't take to the couple at all – maybe because Patch whimpered and shrank away when the man walked towards him. It was funny that was; most of the folk living in the prefab village had called in to see the little dog and he always greeted visitors joyfully with a tail wag.

"It's not wearing a collar," the woman said. "Have you took it off?"

"*He* didn't have one on when we found him," Maisie replied.

"It isn't our dog," the man said. "We've had a wasted journey."

"What a shame," said Maisie, not meaning it at all. "I'll see you–"

She broke off as the twins called from outside. "Mummy, Auntie Arlene's taking baby Christine to the baby clinic to get weighed. Can we go with her?"

"And can we take our dollies in their prams?" asked Dinah as the two of them burst into the kitchen, each holding a walkie-talkie doll.

"Who are you?" Linda asked looking at the couple. "Have you come for Patch?"

"What are you doing, boy?" Dinah asked, putting her doll on the table and walking over to the laundry basket where Patch looked as if he was trying to bury himself under his blanket.

"They thought Patch might be their dog but he isn't," Maisie replied. "I was just going to see them out," she added, indicating to the man and woman to follow her to the front door. To her relief, they followed her quickly.

"I don't think Patch liked them, Mummy," said Dinah as Maisie walked back into the kitchen.

"He certainly looks happier now they've gone. Come here, Dinah and let me brush your hair. You can't go with Auntie Arlene with it all over the place like that."

"I didn't like them, either," said Linda. "I saw that lady looking at Dinah's doll and frowning at her. I think Amelia Jane looks really sweet in the coat you made her, Mummy. Do you like her belt? Dilly found it in the back garden and said we could have it for our dolls."

"It's blue one side and red the other," said Dinah. "Dilly was going to use it for keeping her pen and pencil set in but she gave it to us because, look, it's got–"

"Keep still, Dinah, do," said Maisie, "else I'll have to get Gloria to cut these knots out like she did with Patch."

"I'll get our dolly prams," said Linda. "Auntie Arlene said she'd wait at the end of our lane. And she said to tell you she'll come and see you and Patch on the way back, Mummy."

*

A few minutes after the twins had gone, Gloria called round. "I think someone's coming to see you soon, Patch," she said as the little dog bounded over to her. "Yesterday, one of the char ladies from the Hall said she thought she might know who Patch belongs to, Maisie. She were going to see them last night to tell them to come here."

"A couple came earlier. But Patch wasn't their dog. I must admit I was glad."

"You're getting attached to him, aren't you? I bet the girls are as well?"

"We all are, Gloria. Andy would be made up if we could keep him. And we will if nobody claims him. We haven't told the twins, though. And that isn't why I'm glad Patch wasn't that couple's dog. I didn't like them and Patch looked like he was scared of the man.

"Anyway, have you got time for a cuppa? I was just going to make one before I start on a bit of sewing. It's the Whit walks at the beginning of June and I've got a good few orders for frocks already."

Maisie put the kettle on and reached for the biscuit tin. Patch whined and looked beseechingly at her. "All right, Patch. You can have a tiny bit of *Marie* biscuit."

"I'll bring you a *Bonio* next time, Patch," Gloria told him. "They're special biscuit bones for dogs." Both she and Maisie laughed as Patch wagged his tail.

One cup of tea turned into two and Maisie was about to top up the teapot with hot water yet again, when the twins burst in with their dolly prams, followed by Arlene who looked a bit upset.

"Something wrong?" Maisie asked. "Baby Christine's doing all right, isn't she?"

"She's fine," Arlene said. "But–"

"That horrible lady who came to look at Patch tried to steal my Amelia Jane, Mummy," said Dinah.

"What do you mean? When? How?" demanded Maisie.

"Dinah and Linda left their dolly prams outside the clinic, next to Christine's pram and a good few others," said Arlene. "We got Christine weighed quite quickly so we weren't inside long. When we came out–"

"That lady was bending over Dinah's dolly's pram and was reaching in it for Amelia Jane," Linda interrupted indignantly.

Maisie glanced at Arlene for confirmation. "She did seem about to pick the doll up, Maisie. Your two shouted at her and I asked her what she was doing but she dashed off without answering."

"I'm going to tell Policeman Ken," said Dinah. And she ran out with Linda following before Maisie had chance to stop them.

"I'll make a fresh pot of tea," Maisie said. "You look like you need a cuppa, Arlene. Do you want to fetch Christine in? I mean–"

"I don't think that woman thought there was a *baby* in Dinah's pram," said Arlene. Anyone could see it's a doll's pram. "But I will fetch Christine in. She'll probably be ready for a drink. I haven't got her bottle with me but I got some orange juice at the clinic. I'll make some up and see if she'll drink it off a spoon."

"I don't know what Ken will think when the twins tell him somebody tried to steal a doll," Maisie said while she waited for the kettle to boil again. "It doesn't sound likely really."

*

When the twins returned, Ken Boyce was with them. "Thought I'd come and hear what happened from you, Mrs Whittaker," he said to Arlene.

He sounded quite official using her surname like that and Arlene threw Maisie a worried look. Maisie nodded encouragingly and Arlene explained what had happened.

"Your girls said the woman was the same one who'd been round here earlier with a man, to look at Patch, Mrs Butterworth. Could they be right?"

"Yes. They both saw her when they came running in to ask if they could go to the baby clinic with Arlene."

Ken Boyce frowned. "So the couple knew the girls were going there."

"And the horrid lady looked at Dinah's doll funny when Dinah put it on the table," said Linda.

"Show me the doll, Dinah," said Ken. "And I'll see if I can think of any reason why–"

"Amelia Jane's nothing special," said Maisie. "Well, she is to Dinah but she isn't one of those expensive dolls made for the Coronation or anything like that."

"Here she is, Policeman Ken." Dinah thrust the doll into his hands. "Mummy made her the little coat she's wearing."

"Where did the belt come from?" Maisie asked. "I didn't make that."

"We told you, Mummy. Dilly found it at the end of the garden close to the fence. She was going to keep her pen and pencil set in it but there wasn't anywhere to put them in. She said someone must've made it 'specially for a doll's belt because there's a sort of buckle bit on it. The buckle's broken but that doesn't matter."

"I wonder if it could it be a dog's collar?" said Gloria. "I thought Patch might have–"

"That woman mentioned a collar," Maisie interrupted. "Asked if Patch had been wearing one when we found him. I told her he wasn't and after that the man said Patch wasn't their dog."

"Maybe Patch had a collar and it came off and this is it," said Linda. "We never thought of that 'cos Dilly found it *afore* Gloria found Patch. It was the day Dilly went to stay with Gran; she gave us the belt for our dollies after we'd helped her pack the stuff she was taking with her."

"Do you mind if I take it off the dolly and have a look at it, Dinah?" asked Ken.

Dinah shook her head. "It's a bit lumpy," she said. "Whoever sewed the two long bits of leather together must have made big knots in the cotton. It doesn't matter 'cos the knots are inside and you can't see them."

Everybody watched as Ken removed the belt and ran his fingers down it. "Whatever's making it lumpy it doesn't feel like knotted cotton." He looked at Dinah. "Listen, pet, I think this belt is hollow in the middle and..."

"That's why Dilly tried to find a way to get her pen and pencil set inside," said Linda.

"I want to cut some of the stitches so I can see inside it," Ken said gently to Dinah.

Maisie got some scissors out of the kitchen drawer. "I'll make a new belt for Amelia Jane, Dinah," she said as she passed the scissors to Ken.

Ken cut at a few stitches and then pulled the pieces apart.

"Blimey." Gloria gasped. "Look at that. Her ladyship's bar brooch and little stud earrings. That couple who came to look at Patch must've used the poor dog as an accomplice."

"How do you mean, Gloria?" Maisie asked.

"Well, I bet they made this collar especially for when they went robbing. They'll have undone a few stitches in it before going burglaring, taken Patch with them and put jewels inside the collar through the slit straight off.

"Then," Gloria continued breathlessly, "sewn the slit back up and put the collar on Patch. Even if they'd got caught right after robbing someone, nobody would've have thought to arrest Patch as well. This time though, Patch must've run off while they were stashing the other stuff in the air raid shelter. He likely lived on rabbits for a week. Maybe he'd been catching some regular from near the bramble patch. His collar could have come off one of them times before the day he got all tangled up in the brambles."

"I reckon Gloria used to listen to *PC 49* on the wireless," said Arlene. "He worked stuff out like that. Do you think she's right?" she added, looking at their policeman.

"Could be." Ken nodded. "Now," he said, "I'll need a good description of the couple and then I'll go down to the police station and make out a report."

"One of the char ladies up at the Hall knows who they are," said Gloria. "She told them Patch were here. Not that they wanted *him*. They only wanted the collar with her ladyship's jewels hidden inside."

"So, with any luck we'll soon have those concerned under lock and key," said Ken.

*

"And that was our day, Andy," said Maisie who'd told him everything as soon as he'd got home from work.

"You're sure Dinah and Linda weren't upset about any of it?" Andy asked.

"Ken was really good at how he handled it. I don't reckon they took it on board we'd had criminals here. It was Amelia Jane almost getting taken they talked about most. And of course they're over the moon we're keeping Patch. They can't wait for our Dilly to come home and see him."

"So all's well that ends well," said Andy taking her into his arms and holding her tight.

"Mmm, I reckon so," agreed Maisie snuggling closer still.

An Exciting Blackberry Week

"Auntie Josie, I'm going to call my goldfish Mick because I won him at the Michaelmas Fair," Vivian said, peering at the fish swimming round in the plastic bag. "Or maybe Lolly because he's looking at the ice lolly you bought me off the ice-cream van. It's lovely. I gave Dinah and Linda Butterworth a lick and their mummy's gone to buy them one."

"I think Lolly's cute, don't you, Ruth?" Josie asked her niece's friend.

"Lolly is best," Ruth agreed. "I'm calling my dog Blackberry because it's the Blackberry Week holiday. He's a bit like those dancing dogs we saw in the big tent, isn't he? 'Cept they were real dogs and they were white and mine's a pot dog and he's black."

"I'll put Lolly in a glass jar 'til tomorrow," said Vivian. "Then I'll go and buy him a proper goldfish bowl. And some fish food as well."

Josie smiled at the two excited children. She'd been feeling *proper miserable* when she'd gone round to Arlene's – it had been such a shock when the owners of the pie shop where she worked told her they were closing down. But her older sister always managed to cheer her up.

And, thought Josie, *I'm glad I offered to bring Vivian and Ruth here. I've enjoyed it. And it'll be good stopping the night at Arlene's and going blackberry picking tomorrow. I'll start looking for a new job on Friday.*

*

"I'm glad you're helping us," Vivian said as her aunt dropped a handful of large juicy blackberries into a wicker basket. "There aren't many berries on the low branches and, even if we do piggy backs like Dinah and Linda, *we* can't reach the very high ones."

"I think the three mummies will pick more than us because they can all reach high up," said Ruth.

Josie laughed as she glanced across at her sister who was busily picking with two friends. "They might not *pick* more but they'll have more in their basket because they don't keep eating them like you lot are doing.

"Mind," she added, looking up and down the lane at the groups of adults and children spread out along the many bramble hedges, "I think most folk are eating a fair few."

"That's probably because country lore says blackberries should be eaten before October the tenth because after that date insects spit on them," said Linda. "Auntie Betty told us that."

"The people living in those houses and cottages over there are lucky, aren't they?" said Ruth. "They just have to walk across the road to pick blackberries. We had to walk all the way across Broome Park."

"It only took fifteen minutes," said Dinah scrambling down from her twin's back. "It's taking Gloria and Bernard Turner ages though. I wish they'd hurry up. They're bringing bottles of *Tizer* for all of us and I love that drink."

"I'm going to give Bernard some of the juiciest blackberries as a thank you for giving me a goldfish bowl," said Vivian. "His goldfish died but it hadn't been poorly, it was very, very old. Bernard gave me some special food, too, and I gave Lolly some for her breakfast."

"It feels like ages since *we* had breakfast," said Josie. "I'm hungry and blackberries don't fill you up like fish and chips do. How about I go and get some from that mobile fish and chip shop that's just stopped along the lane?"

"That's a good idea," said Vivian. "We'll come with you and help carry them."

"We'd better wipe the blackberry juice off our hands first," said Josie. "Your mum's put a damp flannel and a towel in Christine's pram, Vivian."

Some of the other pickers had already made their way to the mobile shop and there was quite a queue when Josie and the girls got there.

Josie smiled when a young boy walked by with a black poodle on a lead. "Look, Ruth," she said. "That little dog looks like the pot dog you won at the fair."

"I'm going to ask if I can stroke it," Ruth said and she darted off.

"*I'm* going to ask the fish and chip man if he'll start bringing his van onto Blakeley Road," said Dinah.

"He's called Ray," said Linda. "It says so on the side of the van. *Ray's Fish and Chips*. I like the colour of the lettering. Dark brown looks nice when all the rest of the van's cream."

"Good idea, to ask him to come to the prefab village," said Josie. "He'd need to serve folk a bit quicker than this though or they'd end up blocking the pavement."

"It doesn't usually take this long," a lady in the queue said. "Ray's on his own today. Lost his assistant, he has. He told us that earlier."

Ruth came back just then and she was laughing. "That poodle must have been eating blackberries," she said. "I've got black on my fingers where it licked me. I'll have to wipe my hands again before I eat my chips."

"I hope we get them soon," Vivian said. "I'm starving."

"After we've been served," Josie said, "I want you four to take the fish and chips across to your mums while I have a word with Ray."

*

"It smells wonderful in here, Arlene," Josie said the following morning. "I'm sorry I can't help make the blackberry jam but I've got something else to do, haven't I!"

Arlene, clad in a wrap-around pinny, nodded. "I still can't believe that coming blackberry picking led to you asking for and getting a job on the fish and chip van, Jo."

"I'm right glad you asked me to stop over, Arlene. I'd never have seen the chippy van and heard about Ray's assistant leaving him in the lurch otherwise. He doesn't bring his van round our way."

"Nor here, neither," said Arlene.

"But he's going to start bringing it here." Josie laughed. "Young Dinah Butterworth asked if he would and he said as soon as he'd found a new assistant."

"And he found you a few seconds later."

"And he'll be coming round Broome Park village every Friday, starting this tea time," said Josie. "I'll have got the hang of things by then after doing lunch time in other places. I'd best be off, though, else I'll be late. I'll come back here for my afternoon break, Arlene."

Dinah and Linda arrived with their little terrier on a lead just as Josie was leaving. "We've come to see if Vivian can come looking for two dogs who've gone missing," said Linda. "Then we'll go a couple of doors along and call for Ruth."

"Missing dogs?" Josie asked.

"It's two of the little dogs from the dancing dog act they had at the fair on Wednesday," Dinah explained. "Policeman Ken from the Police Prefab told us last night.

The fair's moved on now but the dogs' owner has left a list of places they'll be at the police station."

"We're going to look in Broome Park," said Linda. "That's where the dogs were last seen *and* it's where we found our Patch when he'd run off from his owners. They didn't want him back, though, so that's how we got him."

"The missing dogs are white," Dinah added, "it should be easy to see them if they're in the park."

"Right. Well, good luck," Josie said. "If Ray's chippy van stops on any of the roads near the park, I'll ask the customers if they've seen the little dogs."

*

The chippy van did stop on a couple of roads near Broome Park and, even though she was kept really busy serving, Josie remembered to mention the lost dogs and asked folk to contact the police station if they spotted them. She kept a look out through the window, too, as Ray drove from one place to another.

"I usually only do Thursdays here," Ray said as he turned onto Blackberry Lane. "But as it's Blackberry Week and folks from all over the area are here picking the fruit I've been coming every day. It'll be time for a couple of hours break after this stop then we'll be seeing if there's any trade to be had in Broome Park village at tea time."

"I'm glad I've got the hang of things because I reckon we'll be dead busy there. I really do."

"You've done well, Josie. It's good how you talk to customers without stopping serving and wrapping their orders.

"Got used to that when I worked in the pie shop," Josie said. "I–"

She broke off as someone came to the serving window and called to Ray, "Are you Joe, Mister?"

"Not me, lad. It'll be her you want." Ray waved a hand towards Josie. "She's called Josie really but I reckon some call her Jo for short."

"Oh right." The young lad was carrying a small pile of newspapers tied with string. "My brother sent you these," he told Josie. "Said you'd be waiting for them special, like."

Josie glanced at Ray and shrugged.

"I always appreciate old newspapers," Ray said. "We use a lot at the afternoon stops when folk are taking their fish and chips home for tea and want them double-wrapped so they'll stay warm longer."

Josie smiled at the lad as she took the newspapers. "Didn't I see you here on the lane yesterday taking your little dog a walk?"

"Isn't my dog. My brother's friend who lives next door is minding it for someone. He don't like dogs, though, so he asked me to take it walks while it's there."

"One of the little girls who was with me yesterday said it had been eating blackberries. Best not let him eat too many, they aren't good for dogs and he might get tummy ache. It looks like you've been blackberrying today as well," she added with a laugh, as she pointed at his black-streaked fingers.

The boy looked at his hands and gasped. "Er, right. Well, I'll be off then." He suited action to words and dashed away.

"Bless him," said Josie, watching him run into a house a little way up the lane. "He had blackberry juice all over his clothes as well. He's probably gone to change before his mum sees the state of him. It's right peculiar about the newspapers, though. I've no idea who he or his brother is."

"No matter," Ray told her. "Like I said, old newspapers are always useful. "Eh up," he added, as a group of children came running towards the van. "Looks like we've a few customers, Josie."

Josie was kept busy serving "Sixpenneth o' chips sprinkled with fish batter," and forgot all about the bundle of newspapers for a while.

But she remembered them when she saw an ice-cream van turning onto Blackberry Lane as they were turning onto the main road. "Joe's Ice-creams and Lollies," she read aloud. "I bet these newspapers were meant for him. If folk buy ice-cream blocks to take home, he'll likely wrap them in newspaper."

Ray laughed. "I'm not turning round and going after him to give him a few old newspapers. Not when it's time for a well-earned break."

Ten minutes later, Josie hopped down from the chippy van at the top of Blakeley Road. "See you back here at five o'clock, Ray," she called before hurrying off.

*

"How did you get on, Jo?" Arlene asked when Josie walked in. "I bet you're ready for a cuppa. We can have one in peace. Baby Christine's asleep and Vivian's round at Ruth's playing in the garden with a few others."

"I saw them," said Josie. "They all seemed a bit sad because they hadn't found the missing dogs. But they cheered up a bit when I said I'd asked folk living in the streets near Broome Park to keep a look out."

"Happen someone will spot them," said Arlene as she passed Josie a cup of tea. "Want some bread and blackberry jam?" she asked. "I made six jars. I left a little bit in the preserving pan and let Vivian and Ruth sample it when it had gone cool. You should've seen the state of them afterwards. All sticky and streaked black they were."

Josie laughed and told her about the lad who'd given her the newspapers. "He had blackberry juice all over his hands and clothes. It was funny about the newspapers, though, Arlene. The lad said his brother had sent them. I rather think he was meant to give them Joe on the ice-cream van – not me on the chippy van. Still, Ray said we use a lot of newspaper at tea times with folk taking their fish and chips home to eat. I hope we get plenty of customers here *this* tea time. I told Ray I reckoned we'd be dead busy."

*

Josie was pleased to be proved right. She hadn't stopped serving for quarter of an hour. And there was still a queue. There weren't any shops in Broome Park prefab village and the folk living there relied on mobile shops. A man with a cart came with fruit and veg once a week and a butcher's van and the bread man came regularly.

"It's good we've got a fish and chip van as well as the others that come. It's just what we needed," said Betty Jones, who lived at number twenty Blakeley Road and told Josie she was *made up* Ray had decided his stopping place would be right outside hers.

"It's about half way along and it's close to Knott Lane as well," Josie said, as she wrapped Betty's order. She glanced over at Ray and told him she needed more sheets of newspaper, then continued her chat with Betty. "Seems fair stopping here seeing as the Butterworths live on Knott Lane and it was Dinah who asked Ray to start coming. I can't see her, though," she added, glancing at the people waiting in the queue.

"I've got the Butterworths' order, Josie," said Gloria. "Policeman Ken's at their place asking if they went anywhere near the ice-cream van when they were at the fair on Wednesday. I think someone else told him that they saw two of the dogs from the dancing dog act near the van. And the ice-cream man wasn't one of the fairground people so I bet he's suspected of taking the dogs away with him when he went. I–"

Gloria broke off as Dilly Butterworth, the twins' big sister, dashed up. "One of the missing dogs has been found," she said. "You'll never guess what. The person who had it had dyed it brown and–"

Everyone started talking at once. But a sudden silence fell after Ray let out a yell, followed by, "I go to the foot of our stairs. Josie, did someone say something about a policeman being somewhere around because I need him here. Pronto."

Josie swung round to ask Ray what he was on about. Then she gasped when she saw the ten shilling, pound and five pound notes spread out on a page in the middle of a newspaper.

"The newspaper's from those the lad gave you," Ray said. "We've been that busy we'd used most of the sheets I brought so I untied this bundle and this was inside the second newspaper I opened. There was nowt like this hidden inside the first one."

"Jeepers," said Gloria, who'd levered herself up to peer through the serving hatch, "some poor soul must've hid their worldly goods inside that newspaper and then forgot they'd done it."

"I don't think *that's* it, Gloria," said Josie. "Now be a love and run and get Policeman Ken from the Butterworths' will you?"

Josie's mind was ticking over fast. She'd said how she reckoned the newspapers had been meant for Joe on that ice-cream van they'd seen. What if it had been him who'd been selling ice creams and lollies at the fairground on Wednesday and driven off with the white dogs and then he'd passed them on to two different people? Dilly said the one that had been found had been dyed brown. Well, the other one could've been dyed black. And if that was it...

"Ruth Whittaker had black on her fingers yesterday after a poodle on Blackberry Lane licked her," Josie told P.C. Ken Boyce a short time later. He'd taken her across to the Police Prefab and Gloria, who'd worked in F.W. Woolworth when she'd lived in Liverpool, had offered to take Josie's place on the chippy van for the evening stops.

"Ruth thought the dog had been eating blackberries," Josie continued. "The lad who was walking the dog, was the one who brought the bundle of newspapers to the chippy van today. He told me he walked the dog for a neighbour, who's minding it for someone. He had black on his fingers and clothes and I don't think it was off the newspapers. He said his brother had sent them and said that I'd be waiting for them special."

Josie took a deep breath. "I didn't know what the lad was on about but I reckon the newspapers were meant for Joe on the ice-cream van and the money hidden inside one of them could have been payment for two stolen dogs."

"Do you know where the lad lives, Josie?"

"I saw him go into a house on Blackberry Lane. I don't know the number, though."

"You'd best come and show me, Josie."

*

"So that's what I did," Josie when she was telling Arlene what had happened. "I had to stay in the police car while Policeman Ken went into the house. The other policeman with us got out and stood on the pavement. Then another police car with two policemen in arrived. They went round the back of the houses.

"Policeman Ken came out and spoke to the one on the pavement. *He* went to the house next door. When he came out, he had the little black poodle with him – only it had white patches on. He said he'd rubbed the fur to see if it had been dyed. Anyway, I think the second two policemen must have arrested whoever they thought guilty and Policeman Ken said some officers had gone to find Joe the ice-cream man."

"What about the young lad, Jo?"

"Policeman Ken said he hadn't known what was going on. He *had* been blackberrying so thought he'd got black on himself that way. His brother told him to take the newspapers to Joe on the ice-cream van but when the lad saw Ray's chippy van which is cream, he thought the brother must have said the cream van. Poor little lad. But his mum was there so he'll be all right."

"Well," said Arlene, "what with you getting a new job *and* helping solve a crime, Blackberry Week's turned out to be a bit more than picking fruit, hasn't it."

Josie nodded. "I hope working on the chippy van won't be as exciting all the time, though."

"I don't reckon anything like what's happened could happen again," said Arlene. "But you never know," she added with a smile.

Penny for the Guy

"So how did you go on at Mrs Double-Barrel's, Pearl?" Alf demanded. "Are you going to be her *Mrs Mopp*?"

Pearl hid a sigh. It wasn't good when Alf referred to the char lady in that *ITMA* programme he used to listen to on the wireless all those years ago. She knew he didn't really like her going out cleaning but it brought in a bit extra.

True, as a warehouseman he came home with a reasonable wage though, with three growing children to feed and clothe, money disappeared fast. Besides, she enjoyed cleaning, especially when it was in a big house with large rooms and a lot of lovely furniture to polish. Take Mrs Moscrop-Jones's for example.

"You should see her place, Alf. The whole of our prefab would fit inside her smallest room with space to spare. I don't know how she's managed without a cleaning lady before."

"Why does she want one now?"

"Her son who's been working away down London for a few years is coming home. She said now there'll be a man about the house again she'll need someone to go in a couple of mornings a week."

"And that someone's you, is it?"

Pearl nodded. "I start tomorrow. I'll be giving the son's bedroom, what's more like a flatlet, a thorough clear out and clean. Mrs M.J. said it hadn't been touched since he left. I'm doing Tuesday and Thursday mornings. Nine-fifteen 'til twelve-thirty."

"Better than working more evenings, I suppose."

She ignored that. It was only the one evening a week she cleaned an insurance company's offices. "Mrs M.J. is paying a bit over the odds, Alf. I'll get my first money just before Bonfire Night so we'll be able to let the kids have a few extra fireworks this year. And one of them big rockets for you to set off," she added with a smile.

Alf laughed. "OK, Bead, love. That sounds all right. And I suppose it'll be good to have a few more shillings in the pot every week."

Pearl nodded. Alf using his pet name for her meant he'd come round. "Talking of the kids, where are they?" she asked. "It's gone six o'clock."

"Bernard Turner off Knott Lane came round with his bogey and they've all gone off to collect wood and whatever else they can scrounge for the bonfire or for dressing the guy. I told them to be back by half-six."

"I popped a shepherd's in the oven before I went for my interview. I'll turn the heat up a bit to brown the spuds. Don't mention anything about extra fireworks," she added. "I want it to be a surprise."

The children got home on the dot of six-thirty. "We've put the wood we collected in the garden shed, Dad," Rob said. "It'll disappear and end up on someone else's *bonnie* if we leave it outside."

"We got loads of branches and stuff," Jimbo shrieked. "But nothing to dress the guy in."

Babs laughed. "He isn't even a guy yet, Jimbo. Just old pillow cases stuffed with straw. We'll see what we can do with him tomorrow."

"So then we can take him out on Wednesday and get pennies for him. And then we'll buy fireworks with the pennies." Jimbo smiled. "It's good fun getting ready for Bonfire Night."

"That's enough chatter for now," Pearl told them. "Go and scrub your hands and be quick about it else the shepherd's pie will only be fit for your bonfire." She smiled as they hurried to the bathroom. They were good kiddies and, although it was money gone up in smoke, she felt right chuffed she'd be able to buy them a few extra fireworks. Hopefully, Mrs M.J. wasn't one of them who didn't pay on time.

*

Pearl glanced round the large bedroom with critical eyes. She'd made a good job of the cleaning and nobody could say different. Except maybe for the carpet. *That* would've come up better if she'd used a *Ewbank* but Mrs Moscrop-Jones had told her to use the vacuum cleaner.

Pearl glared at the nasty noisy thing that looked like something out of space and, to her mind, as about as much use as well. Supposed to float over the carpet like a hovercraft. That was a fib for a start. She'd have muscles the size of melons in her arms if she had to use it too often.

Still, Pearl thought, with any luck Mrs M.J. would be pleased with her efforts in a refined sort of way. She could be a bit la-di-da but she hadn't been too stuck-up to admit she was excited about her son coming to live back at home. He had, she'd said, visited for a day in summer and that made her realise how much she'd missed him.

Ah, this must be her now. Pearl turned as the door opened. "I'm about finished, Mrs Moscrop-Jones. I didn't know if your son might want to keep those?" She pointed to a dozen or so 78 records she'd put on the bed. "A few of them have got scratches on and a couple are chipped round the edges. But if they're old favourites that bring back memories, he might be able to play them still."

"Neville hasn't a single streak of sentimentality in him, Mrs Cole. So they can be thrown out."

"And there's a few shirts and this overcoat I found at the back of the wardrobe," Pearl said. "Looks like moths or mice have had a beano in the coat. I reckon it's beyond repair."

Mrs Moscrop-Jones lifted a sleeve with one nail-varnished finger and nodded. "Only fit for burning."

"There'll be plenty of bonfires in a few days," Pearl said. "All I hear from my three from morning 'til night is, *Can we go collecting stuff for our bonnie* and *have you got any old clothes for our guy*?"

"I presume they will be going out begging with the guy. Mr Moscrop-Jones, bless his soul, would never allow Neville to do anything as common as that. We used to let him have a bonfire in the grounds though the gardener was never too pleased when he had to build it."

Give me a prefab in Broome Park village against this house and its grounds any time if living here makes folk such snobs, thought Pearl as she made a mumbling noise by way of response.

"Anyway, Mrs Cole, it looks very nice in here. Neville is arriving later today so you'll meet him when you come on Thursday. The same time, please. Nine-fifteen."

"Right. I won't be late. Would you like me to put these records in the dustbin on my way out?"

"If you'd be so good. And do take this old overcoat home with you if you think your children might like it for their guy."

"I've not looked in the pockets. There's the two side ones and one inside." Pearl held the coat up. "Perhaps you'd like to look?"

Mrs Moscrop-Jones shuddered delicately. "Oh, I think you could do that, Mrs Cole."

*

"You should've seen Mrs M.J.'s face when I suggested she look in the pockets," said Pearl at tea time as she told the family about her morning. "She must've thought she'd get bitten by a moth or come across a mouse nest if *she* did it. Didn't matter if that happened to me o' course."

"Did it, Mum?" Jimbo looked up from scraping round his rice pudding dish. "If you found a mouse nest, I hope you left it there for me."

Pearl laughed. "Whatever had been living in the coat must've moved on somewhere. All I found in the pockets was holes. And if you scrape that bowl much more, Jimbo, lad, there'll be holes in that an' all."

"Our guy won't mind wearing a holey coat," said Babs, jumping up to clear the table. "Auntie Arlene's given us an old pair of Uncle Cliff's gardening trousers and Bernard's got a jumper for him that used to be Gloria's only it stretched in the wash."

"Bernard uses their big garden shed as a den," said Rob. "We said we'd take the guy there about seven o'clock to dress him. Will that be OK, Mum? We won't be much longer than an hour."

Alf looked over at Pearl. "I told Cliff I'd go to the Woodman's for a quick half, Bead. I'll pick Jimbo up from the Turners' on my way home then Rob and Babs can stay there a while longer if they want."

Pearl nodded. "Be ideal, that will. I'll let my food go down then, with you lot out of the way, I'm going to run a bath, pour in some of that *Youth Dew* you got me for my birthday and have a nice long soak."

Half-an-hour later Pearl breathed in the heady perfume of peach, rose and vanilla as she swirled the bath oil around in the water. When she heard a loud knock on the front door she sighed with exasperation.

Still, at least she hadn't started to get undressed and, hopefully she'd soon get rid of whoever was at the door. It was likely someone trying to sell stuff out of a suitcase. They got a few of them round here.

When she opened the door she saw a tall dark-haired man standing there with a package wrapped in brown paper. He reminded her of someone though, for a moment, she couldn't think who. But when he introduced himself as Neville Moscrop-Jones she realised he had the same facial features as his mother.

"I do hope you don't mind me calling like this, Mrs Cole. Mother gave me your address of course. It's about that old overcoat she let you have for your children's guy."

"You'd best come in," Pearl said.

"Mother told me the coat was full of holes and there were no pockets left and that it was only fit for burning. But the fact of the matter is, Mrs Cole, I always wore that coat when I took my girlfriend out and, well, I'd like it back."

Pearl recalled what his mother had said about him not having a sentimental bone in his body. "You mean you want it back because it reminds you of her?"

"I know that might sound rather silly but she..." He cleared his throat, "She died in a train crash."

Pearl's heart went out to him. "Of course you must have it back," she told him. "But–"

"Look," he indicated the package. "I've brought another coat. I know how important it is to have a guy worth asking a penny for. I used to go *A Penny for the Guy-ing* every year when I was a youngster."

So had Mrs M.J. just been playing Lady of the Manor when she'd said Neville wasn't allowed to do that?

"The coat isn't here, Mr Moscrop-Jones. The children have gone to a friend's. They're dressing the guy there."

Pearl thought he gave a small groan and noticed a look of dismay cross his face. That old coat seemed to be really important to him. Hang on, though. Come to think of it, he looked more annoyed than upset.

"Perhaps you'd be so good as to give me the address, Mrs Cole? I really would like my coat back," he added in an almost bullying tone.

But maybe he was just embarrassed about being sentimental. Saying a silent and regretful goodbye to her anticipated bath, Pearl said she'd get her jacket on and take him round there herself.

*

"It doesn't make no sense to me, Edith," Pearl said a while later as she sat drinking tea in the Turners' kitchen with Gloria and Bernard's mother. "That Neville Moscrop-Jones must have been desperate to get his tatty old coat back. Nobody in their right mind would give an almost new one in exchange when it's to put on a guy what's going to be burnt."

She smiled. "Your Gloria looked a bit taken back when she heard why he was there but the rest of them were right chuffed when they saw the posh coat. They were getting the old coat off the guy quick as quick when I came out of the shed."

"Maybe Mr Moscrop-Jones had left something in one of the pockets," said Edith.

Pearl shook her head. The pockets were full of holes. He knew that. He mentioned his mother had told him."

"Well, perhaps he really did want it for the reason he said."

"And maybe he went out begging for a penny for the guy without his parents knowing." Pearl explained what

Mrs Moscrop-Jones had said about that. "Still, whatever. The kids will have the best-dressed guy for miles around."

"I think we'll get more than a penny for the guy when people see how good he looks," said Bernard who'd just brought everyone into the kitchen for a hot drink.

When Alf arrived to fetch Jimbo he was surprised to see Pearl there and, laughing, put his hands over his ears as she and the children started to tell him what had happened.

Gloria didn't join in and Pearl glanced curiously at her. Usually full of life, was Gloria. Maybe at eighteen she felt past getting excited about guys and fireworks.

But as the Coles left to go home, Gloria said quietly to Pearl, "I'll pop round to yours in the morning. I've something to show you."

*

"I didn't want to say anything in front of Mum," Gloria told Pearl. "She might have got a bit worried. See, Pearl, I cut the shoulder pads out of that old overcoat. The mice hadn't been at them, and I thought I could use them in the duster coat I'm making myself."

"Can't see anything wrong with that, Gloria. Even though we don't have to *make do and mend* any more, it's a shame to let anything usable go to waste."

"But when that Neville fella said he wanted his old coat back I wasn't sure what to do. I mean, they were part of his coat."

"So *that's* why you looked a bit taken back when you heard what he wanted."

Gloria nodded. I'd cut the lining as well, see. The pads were underneath it and it was the quickest way to get them. I felt that embarrassed, Pearl, but I told him what

I'd done. He was stood there holding the coat by then and said he'd like the shoulder pads back.

"Told me his poor deceased girlfriend often used to put her head on his shoulder when he wore the coat because she liked the cushioned feel the shoulder pads gave it. So they were special to him. For a minute, I *almost* believed him. But then, in a right bullying way, he told me to hurry up and hand them over."

"It felt like he was bullying me last night, Gloria, when he asked for your address so he could fetch his coat. But go on, what happened next?"

"Well, I'd shoved them in my pocket straight after cutting them out. When I went to pull them out to give them to him, I felt a bit of paper pinned under the lining material. He was looking all impatient and a bit sort of shifty and I started to think there was something a bit rum about this. I mean someone must've cut the seam of the lining, pinned the paper to the shoulder pad and then stitched the lining back up. And *why* would they do that, 'less it were to hide the paper?

"Anyhow, I fiddled around inside my pocket and moved the lining material so the paper would show when I pulled shoulder pads out."

"And did Neville say anything about the bit of paper?"

"He grabbed the shoulder pads, gave a false hee-haw laugh and said: *I was obviously rather remiss last time I picked up my coat from the dry cleaner's. I forgot to remove the ticket they always pin onto a garment that's been cleaned.* And after that, he hurried off."

Pearl frowned. "They wouldn't have put the ticket under the lining."

"'Course they wouldn't. Anyway, I'd managed to get a good look at that bit of paper as I handed the pads over and it wasn't a dry-cleaner's ticket. It was a ticket for left luggage. And I memorised what was on it and wrote it all down when he'd gone."

Gloria opened her handbag. "*This* is what I wanted to show you, Pearl. The details I wrote down. The station's name was printed on the ticket and there was a signature and a date. N. Moscrop-Jones left something there on August twenty-fifth 1954."

"How strange for him to leave something at a Manchester station when he's been working and living down London for years," said Pearl, staring down at Gloria's neat writing. "Though, hang on, Mrs M.J. mentioned he'd visited her for a day in summer. I don't get it, though. Why–"

"There's more, Pearl, just listen to this."

"Go on." Pearl poured them both a second cup of tea.

"When Dad came home and saw the guy he commented on its posh coat. So I told him how the guy had got it. The name Moscrop-Jones rang a bell with him. You know Dad's a chauffeur for her up at Broome Hall. Well, he said when they had that burglary there a bit back, he heard a newspaper reporter asking a detective if they thought it was carried out by the same gang who were involved in the Moscrop-Jones's burglary a few years previous. There were similarities, apparently, apart from the Moscrop-Jones's house being in the same area."

"I didn't know Mrs M.J. had been burgled. She never said."

"But the thing is, she *was*," said Gloria. "And when Dad told me that, I couldn't help but wonder if the so-called stolen property was in..."

"The left luggage locker what Neville's ticket was for," said Pearl. "But surely Neville wouldn't steal from his mother? He might come over as a shifty character but, oh, I don't know. It's all a bit of a mystery, really."

"I was wondering," said Gloria, "if you and I could go to the station give someone in the left luggage department details of the ticket and say we don't want to take anything out but we just need to check something in the locker."

"I don't think they'd let us do that without the ticket itself," said Pearl. "Besides, whoever's in the left luggage place might remember N. Moscrop-Jones is a man, or he might even know him."

"If that's mentioned we could fib a little bit and say we're related to him," Gloria suggested.

"Wouldn't be right, that wouldn't, Gloria."

"I know. But it'd be for a good reason. And you know his exact address if anyone asks for it."

"Even if they did let us look we wouldn't know if it's stuff from the burglary. And even if we thought it was what could we do about it anyway?"

"We could call in at the Police Prefab after we've seen what's in the locker and tell him about it. He's all right is P.C. Boyce."

"I reckon we should go and talk to him first, Gloria. Let him work out what's to be done. That's if he thinks anything is."

"No sense of adventure, that's your problem," said Gloria, pouting. "But, all right, at least we'll be doing something."

*

Ken Boyce listened carefully to what Pearl and Gloria told him then frowned down at what Gloria had written. After asking a few questions, he said he'd go and make some phone calls. "The Moscrop-Jones's burglary was before my time. I need to check out the details."

"So, seems like he thinks there might be something in it," Gloria said, grinning at Pearl.

Pearl shrugged. If Neville had been up to no good and got arrested or something that'd be goodbye to her new cleaning job because she would've helped lead the police to him. Mrs M.J. certainly wouldn't want her around after that.

"You can leave this to the law now, ladies," Ken said when he came back into the room. Before you go, though, don't you do the cleaning at the insurance office in the town, Pearl?"

"That's right. Once a week. I'll be going this evening."

"What's the name of the big boss there?"

Pearl told him and he thanked her.

"What's the insurance office got to do with anything, though?" she asked.

Ken smiled and tapped the side of his nose.

"Oh, criminy! I get it," said Gloria. "There's only the one insurance office in town and I bet everyone round here with anything to insure uses them. And that'd include the Moscrop-Jones. You think it's going to turn out to be an insurance scam, don't you? That'd make sense. Neville or his mother, or the both of them, claimed for something that hadn't really been taken with the stuff that *was* burgled."

"Don't make sense to me," said Pearl.

"Listen, Pearl. I bet Neville went living down London and took whatever weren't really stolen with him. After he thought enough time had passed he brought it back up here and put it in the left luggage. Then he went off for another couple of months and now he's come back and wanted to get whatever it is and sell it. It's just like a play on the wireless or television, isn't it?"

“And you listen and watch to too many of those programmes, Gloria,” Ken told her. “But as soon as I’m at liberty to tell you anything, I will.”

“He never said I was talking rubbish, though, did he?” Gloria said as they made their way back to Pearl’s to talk about everything again over a cup or two of tea. “I hope he lets us know what’s what soon.”

*

“I never thought for a second Gloria could be right,” Pearl said to Alf two days later. It was Bonfire Night and they, along with most of the other families from the prefabs, were watching the flames gobble up the guy in his posh overcoat and listening to the excited shrieks from the youngsters and the bangs and hisses from the fireworks.

“But like Ken told us this afternoon, she was spot on, wasn’t she?” Alf said with a grin. “Not that we’ll ever know if your Mrs Double-Barrel was involved or if it was just Neville on his own. Still, Bead, you and Gloria look like you might be getting a reward from the insurance company.”

“So,” Pearl said with a giggle, even though my new cleaning job fizzled out and I couldn’t buy extra fireworks for this year, if you’re right about a reward I’ll be able to buy you that big rocket I promised you for next year’s Bonfire Night. But right now, as well as smelling burnt-up fireworks, I’m sure I can smell cooked jacket spuds. So let’s see if we can rake them out of the bonfire because I’m starving.”

Silver Bells, Silver Bells

"Someone's moved in at number two," Gloria said staring across at the prefab opposite. "See, Maisie, there's a light on in the front bedroom. I saw it go on while I was walking round from ours to yours. They must've arrived when it had gone dark though because I was home all day yesterday and never saw a removal van or anything. Strange, that is, moving into a place so late in the day."

Maisie closed the garden gate and waved to her husband, Andy, and their three girls, then watched them go inside before answering. "Perhaps they had a long way to come and it goes dark really early now. It'll be the shortest day of the year next week."

"Then we've got another month or two of wintry weather before it starts to warm up," Gloria said. "It's already cold enough to give a penguin frostbite. I don't really mind, though," she added as they turned out of Knott Lane onto Blakely Road. "I'm that excited about coming to help on your stall. I've never been to Radlington market. Thanks ever so for asking me, Maisie."

"Thank me at the end of the day when you're tired and cold and we're having to lug these suitcases packed with any unsold stock all the way home. The walk from the train station always seems miles long then."

"I doubt there'll be much left. Not if you've run up those kiddies red and green velveteen frocks I saw you cutting out the other day. They'll be perfect for Christmas. Made me wish I was eight again instead of eighteen."

Maisie laughed. "I've got some smashing stuff for the ladies' good as new rail. A couple of the frocks would suit you down to the ground. You'll be glad you *are* eighteen when you see them."

*

"Whew." Gloria let out a deep breath. "You told me the market was close to Radlington station, but you didn't tell me we'd have to walk up such a steep hill to get here. It was harder work than doing exercises along with Eileen Fowler on the wireless.

"Walking on these cobbles isn't that easy either what with the frost and ice making them slippery. But I'm enjoying being here already, Maisie," she added, glancing around.

"Ted Tipper's Tilley boys have brought the lamps round good and early," Maisie said in between greeting her fellow stallholders who called out to her. "Ted's got a warehouse where he lights the lamps and then his boys deliver them off barrows to all the stalls. They come round through the day to pump the lamps up when the pressure starts to fail."

"Is it them I can smell?" Gloria asked sniffing the air.

"They do smell a bit and they sound like a hundred hissing geese an' all. But they give heat as well as light. And it's all part of the market's atmosphere."

"Even though it's too early for many shoppers to be here yet, there's already a smashing atmosphere. I love how there's paper chains and tinsel decorating most of the stalls and some of them have got candy-striped roofs. Don't like seeing them naked chickens and turkeys hanging from the butchers' places though. Where's your stall, Maisie?"

"Right here," she said, pointing to a long stall where, already, there was an attractive display of hats. "Sybil, who makes the hats, isn't up to standing on the market these days so I sell her hats in return for having space on the stall. Sybil's sons, who run the pot stall, see to the setting up and put those ready for me," she added indicating few dress rails.

"We best hurry and get the frocks on them. From the looks of things, folk are spending already. Might be a while before you get a chance to look round, Gloria, but if you want to buy anything you'll get a discount because you're working with me."

*

"I didn't get any discount off the Hot Chestnut Man," Gloria said late that afternoon. "Not like I did at Sid and Duggie's pot stall when I bought a cup and saucer for me mum. But," she added, grinning, "I think Charlie Chestnut put double helpings in the bags. Bursting, they are and the smell's making my tummy rumble. You have a sit down to eat yours, Maisie. There's not that much left here to sell."

"It's been even busier than I expected," Maisie replied as she tucked into the chestnuts. "I'll have to burn the candle at both ends to run up some more of the velveteen frocks to put on the rail tomorrow. Thank goodness I managed to get a lot cut out the other day. And I've got some *Horrockses* frocks to go on the ladies' good as new. I like to put something a bit special out on a Saturday."

"Are you going to bring the kiddies? I bet Dilly and the twins would love seeing it all so Christmassy."

"Andy's on a day off tomorrow so he'll bring them for a couple of hours in the afternoon."

"So is Betty Jones minding them after school today?"

Maisie nodded.

"She might see the new people at number two while she's at yours then. I still think it strange that anybody would move into a place on a winter's night instead of during the day when it's still light."

"You're like a dog with a bone, Gloria." Maisie laughed. "That reminds me. I'll have to go over to Walter's Pet Emporium and get a *Bonio* for Patch. He always expects one when I get home."

"I'll get him one, Maisie. I like giving Patch a treat; he's that gentle when he takes it from your fingers."

"Nothing to do with wanting to see Betty to find out if she knows who's moved in," Maisie teased. "Go on then. You go to Walter's and I'll pack the few things we haven't sold."

*

"Mummy, Mummy, guess what we've been doing?" Dinah and Linda ran into the hallway shrieking together the second Maisie walked in.

Before she had time to answer, Patch bounded over to her and then sat on her feet gazing up at her with big brown eyes.

"Gloria's got your treat, Patch," Maisie told the little terrier. "Go and sit on her feet, there's a good boy. Hello, Betty," she added, as the grey-haired lady came to greet her.

"Hello, Maisie love. You two," she said, looking at the twins and laughing, "let your mum get in properly so she can put her cases down and take her coat off. Then you can tell her all the news while she drinks the cocoa your Dilly's making."

"Make one for Gloria as well, Dilly," Maisie called through the serving hatch once she'd managed to get into the living room.

The younger girls were too impatient to wait until the cocoa was ready. "As soon as we got home from school we went with Betty along Blakeley Road putting posters up on lamp-posts."

"Posters to tell everyone about the party in the Community Centre. Father Christmas will be there and there's going to be singing to Christmas bells."

"It's next Thursday, Mummy, so you won't be going to the market."

"And," said Dilly as she came into the room with cups of cocoa on a tray, "we met someone who's just moved into the prefab over the road who saw us putting a poster on the lamp-post at the end of our lane and came to see what we were doing."

"A grown-up someone or a young someone?" Gloria asked eagerly after thanking Dilly for the cocoa.

"A boy who looks about the same age as me. He told us he lived at number two and then went a bit red when we told him we were from number one. Said he thought we lived on Blakeley Road. He must of seen us at Betty's when we went to fetch the posters."

"Dilly asked him if he wanted to come over here this evening for a game of Tiddlywinks," said Dinah.

"That's all right, isn't it, Mum? It must be horrible living somewhere new at Christmas if you don't know anyone."

"Dilly did say for him to ask his mum or dad first and to tell them you lived opposite," Betty said. "Looked a nice lad. Seemed a bit on the shy side, though."

"I'm not surprised if he had these three chattering at him," Maisie said. "The cocoa was delicious, Dilly," she added, getting to her feet. "I'll get the frocks out of the cases now ready to hang up. They'll get too creased if I leave them there all night."

"I'll help." Gloria jumped to her feet and Maisie hid a smile. Her young neighbour obviously wanted to stay as long as possible in case the boy from number two came over.

"That might be Dilly's new boyfriend now," said Linda giggling as Patch woofed and ran into the hall.

"I'll go and see," Dilly said, hurrying after the little terrier.

"We never did ask him his name," Betty said. "He went off too quick for that."

"This is Graham, everybody," Dilly said when she brought the boy into the room. "He can't stop but his mum sent him to thank us for inviting him."

"Maybe you can come some other time when you've settled in a bit more, Graham." Maisie glanced across at him before lifting a velveteen frock out of one of the cases and straightening the white furry collar as she put it over a chair back with the few others waiting to be hung up.

Graham didn't answer. His eyes seemed fixed on the little frock. "I sell ladies and children's clothes on Radlington market," Maisie told him – thinking he might be wondering why she had all the frocks.

"Would that red one cost very much?" he asked at last.

"Have you got a little sister?" said Linda. "Is that why you want to know?"

Colour flooded Graham's face and he shuffled his feet. "I'm not meant to say," he mumbled.

"Why ever not?" said Gloria. "Is it a secret or–"

"Leave it, Gloria," Maisie said quietly. Holding up a frock to hide her face from all but Gloria, she whispered, "The lad looks upset."

"I'd better go now," said Graham and hurried off before anyone had a chance to say goodbye.

"Bless his cotton socks," said Betty. "He likely felt embarrassed asking about a frock. I'll be off now as well, Maisie," she added. "I promised Tom I'd make cheese and pickle sandwiches for while we listen to *Friday Night is Music Night*."

"Can we have cheese sandwiches as well, Mummy?" asked Dinah, after they'd seen Betty out.

"I'll help Dinah and Linda make them," Dilly offered. "There'll be more room for you to sort the frocks out if we're in the kitchen."

Maisie agreed, glad the thought of cheese sandwiches had prevented the girls from wondering about Graham's words.

"So," said Gloria, "what do you think, Maisie? I'm sure there's something mysterious about them at number two. I mean, why isn't Graham meant to say if he's got a little sister?"

Maisie had wondered about that, too. "It is a bit strange. Maybe his parents are adopting a little girl and she isn't with them yet. Or maybe he's about to have a step-parent who's got a daughter. But it really isn't any of our business, Gloria."

"It would be if they'd kidnapped a little rich girl, Maisie. Broome Park village is a long way from any shops, plus Knott Lane's off the main part. A prefab here would be a good place to keep her hidden away."

"Gloria, I don't know how you think these things up. You should be writing stories for a mystery magazine. Anyway, I haven't time to talk about it any more. I want something to eat and then I'll have to get busy on the treadle if I want something to sell on my Daffy-down Dilly rail tomorrow."

"Right. I can take a hint." Gloria smiled. "I'll see you tomorrow then."

*

Maisie always enjoyed the hubbub of a Saturday afternoon on the market. The stallholders shouted their wares louder than ever and, today, Stan at the record stall put Christmas songs on non-stop. Now, Tony the Toy Man was joining in – playing the tunes on a *Sooty xylophone*.

"When the twins see that, they'll put one on their list for Father Christmas," Maisie said to Andy. He'd arrived with Dilly and the twins, and Graham as well, half-an-hour ago, explaining to Maisie that Graham wanted to buy decorations and presents, too.

"Apparently," he'd added once the children had gone to look round, "Graham met up with Dinah and Linda when they took Patch for a walk and when they told him I was bringing them here he said how lucky they were."

"So they asked if he could come, too," Maisie guessed, nodding. "Taking a leaf out of our Dilly's book, they were. I told you she'd invited him over to ours last night to play Tiddlywinks."

"I sent him to ask his mum and she came over to check I'd offered to bring him. Her name's Peggy Stevenson, her husband's Dan and he's bus driver. He's working so he couldn't bring Graham and Peggy said she'd a lot to do with just moving in."

"Any mention of a little girl?" Gloria asked. She'd obviously been listening to Andy while selling a couple of frocks and a skirt off Maisie's good as new rail.

"Maisie told me about last night and how you both thought there might be a little girl as well," said Andy. "But Peggy didn't say anything about a daughter. Mind, she did seem to be in a hurry to get back."

"Oh, well, I s'pose we'll find out sooner or later," Gloria said. "Perhaps he'll show you what he's bought when you take them for a drink in the café, Maisie. Might be something for his sister. And it's about time you went, they're probably waiting for you by now. I'll try and sell up for you while you're gone," she added.

*

"Oh, good," Dinah said as they went into the café. There's a table in the window with enough seats for the six of us."

"We could do with an extra chair to put all your things on," said Maisie, laughing. "I'd have told you to come back to the stall first if I'd known you'd be buying half the stuff on the market."

"Graham's bought bells, Mummy," Linda said after Maisie had ordered their drinks and *Wagon Wheel* biscuits. "Not the sort where you open the covers and the middle unfolds to make a paper bell. But ones hanging on a pretty string and they really ring when you touch them."

"Real Christmas bells," Maisie said. "That's nice."

"And we've bought–" began Dinah, then she broke off to knock on the window. "It's Joan," she said. "Oh, look, she's seen us. She's waving."

"Is she a friend of yours, Dinah?" Graham asked.

"She's in our class at school. She's our best friend, isn't she, Linda?"

"Are the others in your class friends with her, too?" Graham said.

"O' course they are. Joan makes up really good games."

"Why is she in a wheelchair?"

"Joan had polio, Graham," Maisie told him. "And now she can't walk very well."

"Isn't everyone scared they might catch it from her?"

"She hasn't *still* got it," Dinah said. "But it left her with legs that don't work properly."

"And she doesn't mind people seeing her in a wheelchair? Lucy–" Graham broke off and looked down at the table.

"Is Lucy the sister you're not meant to say about, Graham?" asked Linda.

Graham nodded. "She's seven. She got polio when she was five and, like your friend Joan, Lucy can't walk properly. She has to go in a wheelchair if we go out. But her friends where we lived before stopped being friends with her in case they caught polio and because they didn't like her being in a wheelchair and having braces on her legs. Now she won't go anywhere. She doesn't want anyone to see her or even *know* about her. But she still likes wearing pretty clothes."

"That's why you asked about the red frock last night," said Dilly.

"Mum said she'd buy her a new one for Christmas. Lucy loves that song called *Silver Bells* and we hoped she'd come to the Community Centre to see Father Christmas and sing to the Christmas bells but she got upset when we suggested it. That's why I bought these Christmas bells. It's so Lucy can sing along to them."

Maisie was glad their drinks arrived at that point. Graham, poor lad, needed a moment after his impassioned speech. She glanced at her three girls wondering what was going through their minds.

"If Lucy won't come to Christmas at the Community Centre, we'll have to take Christmas to her," Dilly said. "We'll stand outside your prefab, Graham, so she can see us out of the window but we won't look in at her. We'll just–"

"Dress up in Christmassy clothes, ring Graham's bells and sing Christmas carols to her," said Linda and Dinah together.

"Would you really do that for my sister when you don't even know her?" Graham said.

"We know you, Graham," Dilly told him. "You're our friend now. That means Lucy's a sort of friend, too, and friends look out for each other."

"And," said Dinah, "maybe when you get home today you could tell Lucy about Joan being our best friend and we don't mind the *gallopers* on her legs or her being in a wheelchair. And we wouldn't mind that about Lucy."

"She'll probably be starting at our school after Christmas won't she?" said Linda. "She might be in our class. But even if she isn't, nobody will be horrid to her or leave her out of anything. And we'll play with her at playtime. She and Joan can have wheelchair races."

Maisie met Andy's eyes and knew he, too, must be feeling as if he had a great big lump in his throat.

Later, back at the stall, Maisie took Gloria aside and told her about Lucy.

"So that must be why they moved in when it had gone dark," Gloria said. "The poor little kid not wanting anyone to see her. But it's so lovely what your three are planning to do," she added, wiping away a tear.

"And listen, Maisie. Her up at Broome Hall where Dad works has got a big sleigh thing what a couple of horses pull. She got Dad to check it over the other day because Father Christmas will be riding it to the do at the Community Centre. How 'bout I get Dad to ask if we can borrow it? Dilly, Linda and Dinah could ride in it along Knott Lane so Lucy can look out and see it, then they can jump out by number two and put on their Christmas show for her."

"It's a really smashing idea, Gloria. When we get home, I'll ask Graham to bring his mum over. We need to check everything with her first."

*

At six o'clock on the shortest day of the year, a sleigh lit up with lanterns and pulled by horses wearing bells made its way along Knott Lane and then drew up outside number two. Bright-eyed with excitement, Dilly, Linda and Dinah – all dressed in red cloaks with white fur around the neck and sleeves – jumped out then, with snowflakes tumbling gently around them, made their way up the garden path.

Linda and Dinah had Graham's strings of bells and they shook them to make them ring before they began their medley of Christmas songs and carols. Maisie, Andy, Gloria, her dad Bill and Betty joined in the singing from their seats in the sleigh.

Half-way through *Silver Bells* Maisie broke off. "Look," she said. "Peggy and Graham have brought Lucy out in her wheelchair."

The little girl looked so pretty in her red velvet dress and white furry cape and when Graham leaned over and touched her shoulder, she turned her head to look up at him and nod.

Smiling, Graham moved round and helped her out of the wheelchair. Then, slowly and hand in hand, the two of them walked over to join Dilly, Linda and Dinah. Maisie guessed Graham must have told them to keep singing because their voices rose louder and after a couple of moments, Lucy joined in.

Peggy Stevenson ran down the path and out of the gate to the sleigh. "I can't thank you enough for this," she said, through her tears. "Lucy's been a different child since Graham told her about the other little girl who had polio and how she has friends who don't mind the wheelchair and leg braces. Lucy would like you all to come inside and have something to eat and drink."

"I'll take the sleigh and horses back and join you afterwards," said Bill.

*

"Guess what, Mummy?" Dinah and Linda shrieked half-an-hour later. "Lucy's coming to the Community Centre on Thursday. We're going to push her there in her wheelchair, aren't we, Lucy?"

Lucy smiled and nodded. "I think we'll decorate it with bells and tinsel so it will be a Christmassy ride all the way there," she said.

Knitting for Love

"The first thing I'll do when I get in is have a bath," Gloria said as she and Maisie walked homewards. "Well, the second thing. Granny Turner will be there, I'll have to sit and talk to her for a while first."

"You don't sound very enthusiastic."

"Gran's all right but she knits *all* the time. The clicketty-clack of her knitting needles drives everyone crazy. You can even hear them with the wireless turned up loud. Trouble is, she'll be staying a few days."

"Nobody to hurry home for?"

"No. Her husband went missing years ago. It's a shame really."

"I suppose it was during the war? I used to worry myself sick that my Andy would go missing in action."

Gloria shook her head. "It were back in the late twenties, way before the last war."

"What happened? Did he just go out one day and never come back?"

"Not exactly. He was a Commercial Traveller and worked away. He went home once a month for a long weekend. Dad, he was about fifteen at the time, told us they didn't worry at first when his dad didn't turn up when he was expected. They thought he'd come the next weekend."

"But he didn't?" "No. So they contacted the firm he worked for and they hadn't seen or heard from him for over a month.

They asked around all the commercial travellers' hotels in the areas he worked in but he hadn't stayed in any of them for weeks.

Then they reported it to the police. They circulated details but didn't get any response. Nor was there any from the *missing from home* columns in the newspapers."

"Your gran and dad must've been out of their minds with worry," Maisie said.

"I know. It's impossible to imagine how they felt. Mum thinks, even though it was all ages ago, Gran knits all the time to stop herself thinking about what could've happened to him."

"The poor love," Maisie said, as they started walking again. "She could always come round to ours of an evening, Gloria. What with me at my sewing machine most of the time nobody would notice your gran clicketty-clacking."

"Mum might be glad of that. She'll have had her all day. It won't be as bad for me what with being at work. Talking of work, today was the busiest since I started at the pet shop. I sold so much chicken feed I feel like I smell of the stuff. But I'm right grateful you told me about the job and that you put in a word for me, Maisie. I just wish it wasn't temporary."

Gloria hadn't been at all happy when Mum and Dad told her they were moving to Broome Park prefab village; a place she'd never heard of. *But coming to live here has turned out all right*, Gloria thought now as they turned onto Knott Lane. *Mainly because of having good neighbours like the Butterworths*. Even Maisie's husband, Andy, had insisted on helping them get their prefab straight even though the leg he'd broken a while back still pained him. And, of course, the job in the pet shop was the jam on the bread even though it wouldn't be lasting long.

"I knew you'd be perfect for the job," Maisie said, breaking into Gloria's thoughts. "I'll miss you helping me on my stall but I could tell how much you love animals when you rescued Patch that day. You're good at reorganising, as well. The shop's looking really good now. Walter has always cared for the animals well enough and kept their cages clean but everywhere else was a bit of a tip. Your idea of playing animal songs on that wind-up gramophone was a good idea, too."

"I'll go to Stan's record stall on Friday, see if he's got any new animal songs." Gloria knew she'd blushed when she'd said Stan's name. She really liked him. He was so handsome and easy to talk to as well.

Maisie obviously guessed how Gloria felt. "That's a good enough excuse for going to see him," she said, teasingly. "Be nice if he has got some new records. You play *How Much is that Doggie in the Window* so many times I reckon I hear it in my sleep. But I think the music attracts people to the shop and seeing as my stall is right opposite that's good for me as well. Mind, I'm glad there's no market on Thursdays. I sold so much today I'll be spending all tomorrow making more clothes for my Daffy-Down Dilly rail."

"Bring anything that needs buttons sewing on round for Mum," Gloria said, opening the gate to number three. "She likes doing that while watching television. Gran bought us the television set so we could see the Coronation." Gloria giggled. "She wouldn't have it in her own house, didn't like the idea of television people being able to see her. I don't suppose she'd of bought it if she'd known we'd be moving a few months later and she wouldn't be able to pop in and out of our place all the time."

"She'll have missed doing that," Maisie said. "Just you be nice to her, Gloria," she added as she hurried off.

*

Gloria's mum and gran were in the living room. Gloria went to join them and greeted her gran with a hug and a smile.

"So, how was your day, love?" asked her mum once Gloria had sat down. "Did your new friend, Mr Halifax visit the shop as usual?"

"New friend?" Gran said. "I hope it's nothing serious, Gloria. You're only eighteen."

Gloria laughed. "Mr Halifax is lovely but he's much too old for me, Gran. He calls in most days to look at the monkeys. Says one of his memories is of a zoo in Halifax and looking at the monkeys there. Tells me that every time. That's why I call him Mr Halifax.

"Anyway," Gloria continued, looking at her mum, "Mr Halifax watched the shop for me today while I went to the perfumery stall to buy a bottle of that scented bath oil that's just come out."

"If you're having a bath tonight, I hope it smells nice. Your dad's on nights and you'll be sleeping with me so Gran can have your bedroom."

Remembering what Maisie had said, Gloria glanced at Gran and felt a warm rush of compassion. She vowed she'd try not to let the knitting needle noise get her down. Strangely, though, Gran seemed to be knitting much slower than usual and the noise from the needles wasn't so loud.

"I was telling Maisie on the way home that I must smell of chicken feed. *Youth Dew* will be a hundred times nicer than that, Mum."

"Is there a hairdresser's near this pet shop you work in, Gloria? her gran asked. "My hair needs setting and I want to see your shop. I might as well do both tomorrow."

"You'd be best leaving it 'til Friday, Gran. It's market day in Radlington then and there'll be more for you to see."

*

To Gloria's surprise her gran was up early the next morning. "Ready to come to Radlington with you, Gloria," she said.

It was the same on Friday as well. "I can't understand it, Maisie," Gloria said that afternoon when Walter gave her a break from the pet shop. "Apart from when she had her hair done Gran sat in the shop knitting all day yesterday. I didn't think much of it then, there wasn't that much for her to see. But, even though she said she was coming again today so she could have a look at the stalls, she hasn't budged. She's just sat there all the time. Knitting."

"Maybe she likes the music," Maisie replied with a grin. "Got some new records haven't you? I like that Rosemary Clooney one. *Little Red Monkey*."

"Got a couple from Stan early this morning," Gloria said, hugging herself. "And guess what, Maisie? He's taking me dancing tomorrow night. I need a new dress; that's why I'm here. And to moan about Gran being under my feet. She doesn't even stop knitting when she has to move from her chair to let me reach something."

"Has she really been there all the time since this morning?" Maisie asked as she moved towards a rail of dresses.

"Except from when I took her to the toilets," Gloria said. "You know what Gladys the attendant is like. She leapt to her feet and told us the toilets were for market folk only. Gran said we were from Walter's Pet Emporium and as it was situated on the market place that meant we were market folk.

"Then we were in cubicles next to each other and Gran said loud enough for Gladys to hear: *She's just like that actress Mable Constanduros when she's playing Earthy Mangold Scarecrow in Worzel Gummidge on television*. I'll always think of Gladys as Earthy Mangold now."

Maisie laughed and held up a full-skirted red and white dress with a scalloped neckline. "*You* won't look anything like a scarecrow if you wear this for your date with Stan. You should get your gran to knit you a pretty cardie to go over it. If she really knits all day she could get one finished in time."

Gloria was busy admiring the dress when somebody dug her in the back. She turned to see Walter looking all pop-eyed and worried. "Quick, lass," he said. "Your gran's had a funny turn. That gent who comes in to see the monkeys is there with her but you go to her, Gloria, and I'll run and get some smelling salts from Paddy's Pills and Potions."

Gloria dashed back to the pet shop and found her gran sitting with her knitting on her lap chanting over and over again, "It was the monkeys, the monkeys."

"Gran?" Gloria glanced up at the monkeys in their large cage. They were grooming themselves as usual. "What was the monkeys, Gran?"

"Soon as you mentioned Halifax zoo and monkeys I started wondering. That's why I came and sat here, waiting to see."

"See what?" Gloria wished Walter would hurry with the smelling salts. Gran looked a right funny colour.

"Him of course." Gran waved a knitting needle towards Mr Halifax.

Mr Halifax, Gloria realised, glancing at him when he made a strange groaning noise, was as white as the cockatoo running along its perch.

"It was the knitting that did it," said Mr Halifax.

Gloria thought she'd be the one needing smelling salts if things went on like this. "Did the noise of Gran's knitting needles upset the monkeys?" she asked.

"Don't know about that," the elderly man replied. "It upset me, though. Brought back all my lost memories in one whoosh. Years and years of them."

"In that case, John, you can explain things to me." Gran got to her feet but then sank back onto her chair.

Walter burst in at that moment, strode over to Gran and waved the bottle of smelling salts under her nose. Then Maisie arrived closely followed by Stan.

Stan hurried to Gloria's side. "Someone said the lady in the pet shop had been taken ill and I thought it was you," he said.

"It's Gloria's gran," Maisie told him. Then she looked at Gloria. "Do you want me to run to the telephone box and telephone for a taxi? I think you should get her home quickly."

"No need for a taxi," Stan said. "I'll find someone to see to my stall then I'll go and get my van and take you and your gran home, Gloria."

"What about Mr Halifax?" Gloria said. "He looks proper poorly as well."

"Don't keep calling him that, Gloria," her gran snapped. Clearly, the smelling salts had revived her. "His name is John Turner. He's my missing husband and he'll be coming with us."

Worried her gran was imagining things but would take ill if she said that, Gloria thought it best to let Mr Halifax come with them.

*

It was a quiet journey home. Stan dropped them off outside the prefab and drove off saying he'd see Gloria tomorrow.

She nodded and hurried Gran and Mr Halifax inside.

"Gran says this is her missing husband," she told her mum and dad.

"Look at him, Bill," Gran said. "You must remember your grandad at this age. Your dad's the spitting image."

One look at her dad's face told Gloria that Gran wasn't imagining things.

Gloria had never seen grown men cry before. It made her cry. And her mum as well. "I'll go and make us a nice cup of tea, Mum," she said, wiping her eyes.

"That'd be good," Mr Halifax said. "My head feels strange with all the memories jumping around. It was seeing Emily knitting and hearing the clicketty-clack of her needles that brought them back. Years and years of them suddenly there again but all mixed up. A good strong cuppa might help me get them in the right order."

It was quite a while before everyone settled down enough to hear what had happened all those years ago. Gran and Mr Halifax – Grandad, Gloria supposed she should now call him – were sitting on the sofa holding hands.

"Remember I drove buses when the transport workers were out during the General Strike, Emily?"

Gran nodded.

"Well, one of my regular passengers was always knitting. 'Course I mentioned *you* knitted all the time. She told me she got her wool cheap from a factory in Manchester. So, after that last weekend I came home, I went off to Manchester to buy wool as a surprise for you, love."

"Oh, John." Gran smiled up at him.

"The thing is," his face paled again, "I got set on outside the factory gates. Knocked senseless apparently because the next thing I found myself in a hospital bed with no idea who I was or anything. They told me I'd had no wallet or anything on me when the ambulance fetched me in so there was no way of finding out who I was or where I lived."

"And Manchester was miles away from home," Gloria's dad said into the silence that followed.

His dad nodded. "Not that I knew that, of course. The hospital staff thought I must be married because my ring finger was broken. They reckoned a wedding ring had been forced off it. Anyway, they tried all sorts to help me try and remember something, *anything*, but it were as though I'd never lived before. Mind, I did seem to know what food I liked or didn't like."

"You always hated carrots, John. I bet you remembered that, even though you couldn't remember me or our Bill."

"Sorry, love." Gloria saw his eyes fill with tears again. But he went on talking fast without hardly drawing a breath. "The doctors said something might happen one day to bring my memory back properly. Anyway, they decided to call me John Smith. Funny that, as John was really my first name but I didn't know at the time. I used that name when I left the hospital. The hospital almoner helped me find a job and a place to live. I was taken on as a warehouseman in a factory in Stockport.

"When war came I stayed there doing war work and after I went back to being warehouseman there until I retired a couple of years back. Then I moved to a place a few miles away from Radlington and spent my time wandering round local markets. Don't ask me why. I suppose it were just something for a lost soul to do."

"But in all that time since you were robbed didn't you *ever* remember anything of who you really were?" Gloria asked.

"He's getting tired, Gloria. Don't keep on at him," said her dad.

"It's all right, Bill. It was seeing the monkeys in the pet shop she works in that made me remember seeing monkeys at a zoo in Halifax, though I couldn't recall what age I saw them. That's why I kept coming most days, Gloria, to see if they'd help me remember more."

"And Gloria told me about this man who talked about Halifax zoo and monkeys," Gran said. "That's why I came and sat in the shop. Knitting and waiting for you to come. I reckon my heart knew it had to be you, John. You and me met at that zoo. You were working there. Stayed there after we married, you did, until it closed down."

"And that's when I had to take a job that kept me away from home most of the time. I didn't write to you, either, during the weeks I was away. I should have. But, Emily, love, how on earth did you manage when I went missing?"

"Never mind that, now. I'll tell you when we go home. I don't live here. Home is still where it was, John, over in Liverpool."

"Home is where the heart is," he said. "I reckon you and our Bill were always in my heart, Emily, even when I couldn't remember a darned thing."

"And now you've got me and Mum to fit in your heart as well," Gloria said, going over to hug him tight.

"That makes me very happy," he said. "But is there any chance I could go and have a lie down? I think I need a right good sleep."

"Our Bernard is sleeping at his friend's tonight. You can use his bed," Gloria said.

Gran shook her head. "We'll use Edith and Bill's bed, John. Edith can share Gloria's for one night and Bill can sleep in Bernard's bed."

"That'd be lovely, Emily. But for heaven's sake don't bring your knitting. Not tonight love."

*

"And that's how the evening ended," Gloria said next morning in the pet shop after telling Stan, Maisie and Walter her grandad's story. "It was lovely," she added. "You could tell him and Gran still love each other."

"Love's what makes the world go round," Stan said, winking at Gloria. "Now I'd best be off and get my stall set out. I'll see you later."

"Sounds and looks like the world will be going round for you and Stan, Gloria," Maisie said before she, too, hurried away to her stall.

Gloria smiled. She felt sure Maisie was right.

Gloria's Errand

"Your Bernard worked hard today, Gloria," said Maisie. They were walking homewards along Blakeley Road, each carrying a case containing the few items that hadn't been sold on Maisie's market stall.

Gloria nodded. Although she loved her younger brother they didn't always get on. Their mum said that was because they were both at a difficult age. Bernard at just thirteen wasn't sure how grown-up he should act and Gloria at nineteen behaved as if she were Bernard's age one minute and a responsible adult the next.

Whatever, Gloria had felt a bit doubtful about Bernard coming to the market to try and earn some money for his scout troop's *Bob-a-Job week*. She worked there; it wouldn't look good if she and Bernard had one of their quarrels.

But it had all gone well. The two of them hadn't argued once and, best of all, the stallholders had found Bernard quite a few jobs to do – some of which had been quite messy.

In fact, she'd been so proud of him she'd even lent him some money to buy some roller skates from Tony the Toy Man. Bernard was trying them out now – roller skating along the pavement. Though amazingly, still on his best behaviour, he had offered to carry the cases first.

"No prizes for guessing how he'll be spending his time during the rest of the school holiday," said Gloria. "It's a long one this time. Easter's over a week away yet and they don't go back until the middle of April."

Maisie shook her head. "March has gone really fast. It's hard to believe it's April on Friday."

"Remember I won't be coming to give you a hand on the stall," said Gloria. "I'll be up at Broome Hall with Mum serving drinks at her ladyship's lunch-time cocktail party."

"She has one on the first Friday of every month, doesn't she?"

"Yes. It's a sort of tradition, I don't know why. Drives Mum crazy having to do it. She'd rather be behind the bar at the Woodman's. But because her ladyship buys her supplies there, the landlord had to agree when she asked for Mum to go and do the serving and waiting on.

"It drives me crazy an' all going to them cocktail dos. I don't like missing a day at the market." Gloria sighed. She loved working on Maisie's *Daffy-down Dilly clothes for Ladies and Children* stall.

"You mean you don't like missing seeing Stan on his record stall," Maisie said, teasing her younger friend. "At least on Friday me, and the other market folk, will get a break from hearing him play that Ruby Murray record," she added laughing. "He plays it as a message to you, Gloria, I'm sure he does. Never takes his eyes off you while it's on."

"You mean *Softly, Softly*," said Bernard who'd roller-skated back to them in time to hear Maisie's words. "Can't imagine Stan would want Gloria to open his heart with a key. Though she'd likely be soppy enough to try."

"Any more of that and I'll take those skates and not let you have them until you've paid back the money I lent you," Gloria said. She meant it, too. She was annoyed that her pest of a brother had spoilt the moment for her. She'd been right chuffed to think of Stan playing that record to send her a love message.

It was strange really because if Stan liked her so much, why hadn't he asked if he could take her to the pictures or somewhere? Surely he wasn't shy?

"If you touch my skates," said Bernard, interrupting her thoughts, "I'll tell Mum you were moaning about doing her hair tomorrow."

"If you two can stop argufying for a moment," Maisie said, as she stopped outside Betty Jones' prefab, "I'll say goodbye. Betty said she'd bring the girls here instead of minding them at mine because they like watching *The Grove Family* on television. Plus, Andy's on nights so he'd have been able to catch up on his sleep better without the girls there."

"Tell them I'll give them a go of my roller skates tomorrow," said Bernard.

"I won't mind Dilly having a go," Maisie said. "But I think those skates will be too big for the twins."

"I never thought of that," said Bernard. "But Dinah and Linda can watch if they want."

"Do you need me for anything tomorrow, Maisie?" Gloria asked. When the market wasn't on, she often helped Maisie with dress-making or repairing clothes for the *Good as New* rail.

"Well, I've a dozen new dresses I've made that need buttons sewing on."

"I'll come round after I've done Mum's hair then. I just hope this new *Twink* perm turns out all right."

Maisie opened the gate. "If Edith's looks good maybe I'll let you perm mine next week. I wouldn't mind a curly hairstyle for Easter," she added as she hurried down the garden path.

"If Mum's hair turns out awful, Gloria, she'll be hopping mad," said Bernard as the two of them made their way towards Knott Lane and home. "But I'd lend you my skates so you could get away fast," he added with a cheeky grin.

"I wouldn't mind a go of them some time," Gloria said remembering Marilyn Monroe roller skating with Cary Grant in the film *Monkey Business*. If she could look just half as good as Marilyn had, she'd make sure Stan was around when she had a go. Maybe then he would ask her out.

*

"It smells like rotten cabbage in here," said Bernard pulling a face as he walked into the kitchen where Gloria was perming their mum's hair. "Perhaps it's a bit like medicine. You know, the worse it smells, the better it is for you. I was going to make myself a jam butty but that smell's put me right off."

"It's only half-an-hour since you had breakfast, Bernard. You can't be hungry again."

"I wouldn't be if you'd saved me more *Shreddies*, Gloria. There was hardly any left in the packet. Weren't even enough to fill half a bowl."

"You should've been here on time for breakfast then instead of roller skating up and down Knott Lane showing off to Graham Stevenson. Heck, Mum, keep your head still, it's hard enough winding your hair round the rod things without you moving all the time. I'll have to unwind this one and do it again now and, at this rate, I'll run out of these paper bits."

"I'm trying to turn the wireless up to drown out the noise of you two squabbling," said their mum. "It's George Elrick compering *Housewife's Choice* this week and he's my favourite."

"Ooh and just listen what record he's playing," Bernard said gleefully. "It's that soppy *Softly, Softly* and our Gloria will make a right mess of your hair now what with dreaming of him on the record stall. "What's he called again, Gloria? Stan, isn't it. You're hoping his love will–"

Gloria threw down the tail comb and, grabbing a lump of cotton wool, strode over to her brother. "One more word from you and I'll block your mouth with this," she told him.

"That's enough, you two." Their mum stood up and the towel from around her shoulders dropped to the floor. "Bernard, get yourself outside and don't come back 'til dinner time."

"But, Mum–"

"I mean it, my lad. Move."

Bernard did as he was told but not before muttering to Gloria that he'd get his own back on her.

Sighing, Gloria picked up the towel, shook it and put it back over her mum's shoulders. "I reckon all the horridness he didn't use yesterday is coming out today." Then seeing the expression on her mum's face she nodded. "All right, I was just as bad. I wouldn't really have stuffed cotton wool in his mouth, though, and he knew it. So he needn't have threatened to get his own back."

"I don't suppose he will, Gloria love. Now let's forget it so you can get the rest of the curlers in my hair, else the bits you've already finished will be turning to frizz."

*

"Well, Edith. Your hair looks a treat, love."

"You really think so, Bill?"

"I do. You'll outshine her ladyship and her friends at tomorrow's cocktail party."

Gloria laughed as her mum pulled a face. "We were just saying before you came in, Dad, that we wished tomorrow was over and done with."

"I reckon, secretly, her ladyship feels the same way. Seems to get herself in a right flap about it. Going doolally when I left because she couldn't find the earrings she's planned on wearing. Even had me searching down the back seat of the Rolls in case they'd somehow got there. As if I wouldn't have found them if they'd been there."

Gloria smiled. Her dad was her ladyship's chauffeur and took great pride in having the car shining to perfection both outside and in.

"She'll have to set our Gloria onto finding them," Bernard said. "She likes playing detective, don't you, Sis?"

"I just like using my brains," she replied, determined not to let Bernard rile her again.

"And I didn't see you turning up your nose when your sister shared some of the reward money she got for helping detect an insurance fraud," said their mum.

"That's right enough. I suppose it's not too bad having a sister like her." Bernard grinned and pulled something out of his pocket. "Here, Gloria, I bought you a *Wagon Wheel* to make up for getting at you earlier. I know they're your favourite biscuit," he added.

"Thanks, Bernard. It's not too bad having a brother like you, either," she said. "I'll save this to have with my bedtime cuppa. Right now I'd best pop next door, else Maisie will think I've forgotten I said I'd sew buttons on the dresses she's made."

"It's almost six o'clock," said Bernard. "Our patrol leader will be home from work now. I'll go round to tell him how well my Bob-a-Jobbing went at the market yesterday."

They left the room together and grinned at each other when they heard their mum say, "Isn't it nice to see the pair of them being friendly to each other, Bill?"

*

When Gloria got up the next morning, her brother was the only one around. She'd overslept a bit because she'd stayed late at the Butterworths' the previous evening. Maisie liked a bit of company when Andy was on a night shift.

"Mum's already gone up to Broome Hall," Bernard said. "And Dad went early as well. He called back here to give you a message, though. He wants you to do an errand for him, well, for her ladyship really. He's got to go and fetch one of her friends and he might not have time to do it himself."

"I hope it isn't going to *Affleck and Brown's* for fancy tablecloths like last time Dad sent me on an errand for her."

"No. Remember how Dad said she couldn't find the earrings she wanted to wear today? She remembered where they are. At the jeweller's being repaired. So she wants them collecting and needs them before twelve because that's when the cocktail thing starts.

"Here," Bernard handed her a piece of paper. "Dad's written the address down for you. It's not in town, you won't even have to go on bus. It's a small shop on the main road near that place where they have dances. He said they'll be expecting you because her ladyship telephoned and told them."

"Right. I'll just have time for a quick cuppa and a piece of toast before I go then. Honest to goodness, why can't her ladyship be better organised?" she added, putting the kettle on to boil. "Or why couldn't she have worn a different pair of earrings?" she asked as she cut a thick slice of bread. "She must have loads of pairs."

"Dunno." Bernard shrugged. "Folk like her act different to folk like us, I suppose."

"Mmm. Shall I do you a piece of toast as well, while I'm at it?"

"No thanks. I'm going over to call for Graham. I was only waiting to give you the message from Dad."

Gloria ate and drank quickly, rinsed her plate and cup under the sink and then hurried out.

It was a lovely spring day and the scent from the daffodils and other flowers in the prefabs' front gardens filled the air. She smiled as she passed the village's younger children playing out – kicking balls around, or pushing their dolls' prams up and down Blakeley Road.

This is much better than spending the whole morning indoors up at the Hall, she thought, as she turned onto the main road. Shame, really, it would only take her another fifteen minutes or so to get to the jeweller's shop.

*

As Gloria pushed open the door of the small shop, someone from inside yelled "Stop him. He's a thief."

Without thinking, Gloria grabbed hold of the wiry-looking man about to step out. He struggled and kicked out at her and wriggled out of her hold. He ran a few yards down the street but Gloria had turned quickly and was catching him up.

With a wild whoop she threw herself at him in a sort of rugby tackle and the pair of them hurtled to the ground.

"Well, done, Sis. Keep him there. I'll sit on his legs so he can't get up."

"Criminy, Bernard. What are you doing here?" Gloria said, gasping a little as her brother sat on the man's legs, placing roller-skated feet firmly in the small of the man's back.

"Tell you later," he said as a few people came running up – one of them shouting the police were on the way. "Are you all right?" he added, looking anxious. "You're not hurt are you? If you are..." He lifted one foot then thumped it back down hard on the now still and quiet man's back.

"Here, love. You and the lad get up. We'll take care of this good for nowt now."

Gloria glanced at the two well-built fellows who were standing close and, nodding, rose to her feet. Bernard got up, too, and seeing his worried look, Gloria smiled reassuringly.

Before she could say anything, a young man who looked round about her age hurried up. "I didn't mean for you to chase him and put yourself in possible danger," he said. "It was me called out to you to stop him," he explained. "I work in the jeweller's. I was there on my own, Mr Simmonds who owns the place doesn't come in on Fridays. That man there came in and tied me up before filling his pockets with rings and brooches from the small display board I was arranging on the counter. And–"

"Never mind that now," said one of the onlookers. "You ought to sit her down with a cup of strong, hot tea. And here come the police. You get to the shop and make her that drink. They'll know where to find you."

Gingerly holding Gloria's elbow, the jeweller's assistant led her to the shop with Bernard roller skating alongside. To her amazement as soon as they stepped inside the young man spoke to her brother.

“Get those skates off, Bernard, then go through to the back and put the kettle on. It boiled a bit earlier so it won’t take long to boil up again. You’ll see everything there you need to make a cup of tea.”

“Do you know my brother then?” Gloria asked once she was sitting on a chair behind the counter.

“I’m his scout patrol leader and I’m sorry I let him talk me into it now. But neither of us knew there’d be someone here tying me up and thieving goods.”

“Talk you into what?” Gloria wondered if she’d banged her head when she’d tackled the thief to the ground because she couldn’t understand what this man was on about.

Bernard came through from the back with a cup of tea. Pushing it into Gloria’s hands he said, “You do know what date it is, don’t you?”

“Friday the first of April 1955. There. I haven’t had my sense knocked out of me.”

“Right. So what happens on the first of April, Gloria?”

“Folk play... Bernard. You mean that man wasn’t really a thief? It was an April fool joke?”

“No. He was real enough,” the young man said grimly.

“Coming to get the earrings was a fool’s errand,” Bernard explained. “See, I got the idea when Dad were saying her ladyship couldn’t find them. I knew Brian worked here and I fixed it with him. When you asked for the earrings, he was going to hand you a bit of paper with *April Fool* written on it.

“And I’d followed you all the way and was going to come in and watch your face when you got handed the paper.”

“It’s there ready.” Brian pointed under the counter and Bernard picked the piece of paper up and handed it to Gloria. "I'm really, really sorry," Brian continued. "I never dreamed anything awful could happen."

"Well, it didn't really, did it?" said Gloria. "Because of Bernard sending me on a fool's errand I was here at the right time so it turned out lucky in the end."

"Smile, please." The voice came from the door and Gloria glanced over to see a man with a camera. "Local newspaper reporter. The paper's due out tomorrow and I reckon you'll be on the front page," the reporter said.

Things seemed to happen fast after that. Bernard told the reporter the whole story and Gloria and Brian had to give a statement to the police.

It was mid-afternoon before Gloria and Bernard got home and when their mum heard what had happened she clearly didn't know whether to tell them off or hug them because they'd kept safe.

After *ooh-ing* and *aah-ing* a while – and adding her ladyship had found her earrings, they'd been in her jewellery box after all – she sent Gloria for a warm bath and told her to go for a lie-down afterwards and she'd bring her a nice cup of tea and some dainty sandwiches and hors d'oeuvres she'd brought back from the cocktail party.

"Give our Bernard some, too, Mum. He was a real hero sitting on that thief the way he did."

*

Gloria had an even better reason to feel pleased with her brother the next day when she was working on the market. Because if Bernard hadn't sent her on the fool's errand, the story of how she'd put herself in possible danger by running after and apprehending a thief wouldn't have appeared in the local paper.

Stan wouldn't have read the story so wouldn't have come running over to Maisie's stall to check Gloria was really all right. And hugging her when she assured him she was.

And we wouldn't have been here at the pictures watching *Happy Ever After*, Gloria thought that evening. And I won't have to have a go on Bernard's roller skates to try and get Stan's attention, she mused contentedly as Stan's arm crept around her shoulder. Because I've a feeling the two of us will be happy ever after as well.

Something Mysterious at Broome Hall

"I'm not used to being head organiser of big events, Gloria," Edith Turner muttered.

She glanced around their living room at the prefab villagers who'd come to discuss the Easter Fun Day being held in Broome Hall's grounds.

Gloria smiled. "That's down to Dad, really, isn't it? What with him being chauffeur up at Broome Hall everyone thought you'd be the best one to liaise with her ladyship. They were right an' all, Mum. Everything's gone well so far."

"I suppose," Edith agreed. This was the last meeting until the day itself and she hoped it would run smoothly.

"Right, everyone," she called. "The count-down starts tomorrow morning with the making of paper mâché eggs and Plaster of Paris Easter bunnies in Broome Hall's big barn. They'll be left to dry overnight and the next day they can be decorated ready for the competition on Thursday.

"Which," she added, laughing, "as you all know is Fun Day. The judging will take place first thing."

"Is it right her ladyship has got an actor off television coming to judge the competition and award prizes as well, Edith?" someone asked.

"It is. Then after that, we'll be selling our decorated eggs and bunnies and other Easter goodies as well.

"There'll be singers and a rock 'n' roll band performing. It's been advertised in the local newspapers for the last three weeks now. So, hopefully there'll be a lot of people paying for entry into Broome Hall's grounds to see them and to spend at our stalls."

"You'll be glad to know our hens are laying well," Mary Clayton said. "So I'll have plenty of fresh-laid eggs to sell."

"That's grand, isn't it, Edith." Bill smiled at his wife. "I reckon, one way or the other, there's someone from every prefab in the village playing a part."

"'Course there is, Dad," said Gloria. "It might all be happening in Broome Hall's grounds but, except for her ladyship getting the actor and the singers and letting us use the barn and grounds, it's us lot done all the planning and organising."

It was almost midday before they'd finished going over the plans and making sure they all knew who was doing what.

Edith gave a sigh of relief after she'd seen everyone off. Still, she thought, everything seems to be in hand and, hopefully, there'll be a goodly amount of money raised to go towards the building of Broome Park's children's holiday home.

"I've just time for another cup of tea, love," Bill said. "Then I'm to go to the station and fetch that reporter who'll be stopping at the hall.

"Her ladyship was chuffed to pieces when he phoned her to ask if he could come along to do write-ups and take photos and of everything from start to finish. He'll be taking photos of her Russian egg jewellery as well and no doubt there'll be a big picture of her wearing it in the posh glossy magazine," he added, smiling at Gloria.

"There's already been photographs of it in magazines," said Gloria. "I've cut them out and I'm taking them to the barn on Wednesday so we can get ideas for decorating our paper mâché eggs."

"There's a couple of her ladyship's friends arriving this afternoon as well, Edith." Bill nodded his thanks for the cup of tea she handed him. "I've volunteered you and Gloria to go and give a hand getting their rooms ready."

"I'll check up on our Bernard, too," Edith said. "He and his friends are up there getting the big barn ready for tomorrow. It's good for the youngsters having something to keep them out of mischief during the school holiday."

Gloria laughed. "They'll enjoy themselves even more tomorrow, blowing up balloons and sticking strips of paper on them to turn them into eggs and making a mess with Plaster of Paris to pour into the rubber moulds."

"We've got a couple of dozen moulds for making the Easter bunnies, I hope that'll be enough," said Edith. "And I hope all the youngsters understand they won't be keeping whatever they make and everything will be going on one of the goods for sale stalls."

"They can always buy their own bunny or egg off the stall, Mum. I reckon a few of us will be doing that."

"Stop worriting, Edith," said Bill. "Her ladyship's going to hand out a chocolate egg to every youngster who makes something. They'll appreciate that more than an egg or rabbit they can't eat. Everything will be fine. You wait and see."

*

The next morning, Gloria was hurrying down Blakeley Road when she heard someone calling from one of the prefabs.

She turned to see Janet Whittaker hurrying towards her.

"I'm going up to Broome Hall to help get sandwiches ready for those who are making the eggs and rabbits in the barn," said Janet. "Are you going yet, Gloria? If you are, I thought we could go together."

"I was up there before the Claytons' cockerel crowed checking everything was laid out ready in the barn," Gloria replied. "Then I had an errand to run. I'm on my way back to the hall now. I'm going down Broome Avenue and over the stile into the park. It's the quickest way, walking across the fields."

"Are you on the sandwich-making rota, too?"

"No. I'll be in the big barn, making an egg. I saw a photograph of her ladyship's egg pendant in a magazine so I want to make a tiny egg and tomorrow I'll decorate it like the one on the pendant. I can't wait to start it, but I had to go and buy herring roes for Tai-Lu."

"Tai-Lu? You mean a live version of the cat in those stories on television? Is it one of the actors who tell the stories judging the contest?"

"No, it's an actor who had a part in *The Grove Family* doing that. One of her ladyship's guests has named her Siamese after the storybook one. Her ladyship ordered roes specially, but when they checked the delivery they were cod roes and Tai-Lu won't eat them."

"I'm glad I saw you," Janet said, following Gloria over the stile. "I'd be nervous arriving on my own what with her ladyship having special guests stopping there to take part in things."

"There's only the reporter from the glossy magazine, who talks like he's a plum in his mouth when he speaks to her ladyship, and two or three of her ladyship's friends at the hall yet. One's the owner of the fussy Tai-Lu."

"So when are the stars coming?"

Gloria had heard the details from her mum so many times she knew them off by heart.

"The actor's coming tomorrow afternoon and staying at the hall overnight. The Lady Mayoress, the singers and the rock 'n' roll band will arrive early on Fun Day. I'm hoping to get autographs of all them in the rock 'n' roll band."

They chatted about the band until they reached the hall.

"I'll bring these in for Tai-Lu," Gloria said, "and then go and get on making my egg."

"Shall we walk home together as well, Gloria?"

"Could do. I won't be leaving early, though. I said I'd stop behind and tidy the barn when all the making of everything's over."

*

It was five o'clock before everyone hurried out of the barn to go home. Gloria heaved a sigh of relief. Now she'd be able to set to and clear up the mess.

The paper mâché eggs and the plaster bunnies, the filled rubber moulds suspended over small jars, had been set out neatly on a large table to dry. But the floor and other areas were covered with torn paper, flour and water paste and powdered plaster.

Half-an-hour later, she'd just finished wiping the old wooden work benches when Janet came in with Tai-Lu on a harness.

"Her ladyship asked me to take Tai-Lu for a walk," she said. "She's putting on a big dinner for her guests and they're all getting changed. I had to go and fetch Tai-Lu from her owner's room and I felt a right twerp when I realised I was walking along the wrong corridor."

"It's such a rambling old place, it's easy to lose your way in it," said Gloria.

Janet nodded. "Even that reporter man did that this morning. I was taking a cup of tea up for one of the guests and I saw him outside her ladyship's rooms looking very flustered. I reckon I startled him because he almost dropped his camera when he noticed me there.

Said he was looking for his room to fetch a new roll of film."

"He took loads of photos," Gloria said. "He made a bunny, as well. Got in a bit of a mess," she added, laughing. "I don't think he's ever poured Plaster of Paris into a mould before.

"Anyroads, Janet, we'll never get home if we stand here chatting. So you'd best take fuss-pot here for a walk and I'll sweep this floor."

"I've already walked her around the grounds. I came to see if you were nearly ready to leave."

"I will be when I've swept the floor."

"If you've got another broom, I'll help," Janet offered. "It'll get done quicker with two of us."

Tai-Lu jumped elegantly onto the larger table.

"You might be a fussy eater, but you're a clever girl putting yourself out of the way," Gloria said, stroking the cat's head.

A few minutes later as Gloria was dropping the sweepings into a sack, there was a small crash followed by a yowl from Tai-Lu.

"Jeepers," said Gloria. "She's knocked a jar off the table and the rubber mould has come out of it."

She hurried over to pick it up. "It's Jeremy-the-reporter's bunny," she said, pointing to the piece of paper stuck on the mould. "The moulds are all the same so we put our names on them to make sure we paint and decorate the right one tomorrow.

"I think the plaster has cracked," she added, feeling the outside of the mould.

"No, it won't be dry enough yet to have cracked," said Janet.

"It will. We added salt to the plaster and used warm water to mix it so it would set really quickly. Oh, it's a shame. Jeremy isn't so bad when he forgets to try and talk posh."

"You could empty it out and make another one," Janet suggested.

"There's no Plaster of Paris left," said Gloria. "Tell you what, though. We've got some at home. I'll take this mould with me." She put it into her skirt pocket. "I can refill it there and bring it back in the morning."

"What if Jeremy comes in here before you get here and notices his is missing?"

"Good point, Janet. But I made a bunny as well as an egg. So," Gloria looked for the rubber mould with her own name stuck on it. "I'll take my name off and stick Jeremy's on. It's not like cheating because the competition is for the best painted and decorated bunny."

Janet laughed. "Good job *this* Tai-Lu can't talk like the storybook one. I'll take her in now, Gloria, and then we'll get going."

Her ladyship always insisted on all the outbuildings being locked at night in case any passing tramp thought of making a bed for the night in one of them. She'd given Gloria a spare key so, after carefully locking the barn doors, Gloria put the key in her pocket and then waited for Janet to return.

*

When Gloria got home and explained what had happened, Bernard asked if he could mix the plaster to refill the rubber mould.

"I need to empty the mould first," said Gloria.

"Cover the worktops with sheets of newspaper before you do anything else," said her mum who was on her way to work at the Woodman's Inn. "I don't want the pair of you messing up my kitchen."

Bernard spread out the newspaper and Gloria pressed the top of the rubber mould.

The bottom half of the rabbit shape dropped out.

"Thought so," Gloria said. "It's broken in half, or maybe into three."

"It's a blinking good job you realised the plaster had cracked," said Bernard. "That snotty reporter would have likely hit the roof if he'd released his bunny from the mould and it had come out broken in front of everyone."

"He's OK really, Bernard."

"Huh! You didn't hear him telling me off for disturbing him. And I were only–"

Knowing her brother could go on for ages about things, Gloria interrupted him. "Here's the next bit dropping out, see. Hang on, what the heck?"

Gloria stared down at a small cellophane package.

"Jiminy. It looks like her ladyship's egg pendant wrapped up in this. It *is*," she said looking closer.

"Don't take it out, Gloria. There might be fingerprints on it. It was a right clever idea to hide it in the plaster, wasn't it? When her ladyship discovers its missing and phones the police they'll search everybody's room and find nothing. They'd never think of looking–"

"Stop yattering, Bernard, and run and fetch Policeman Ken from his prefab. He is in, I saw him when I was coming home. Then go and get Janet. She saw something earlier that the police need to know about."

"And she isn't the only one," said Bernard as he hurried out.

*

"So, Gloria," said P.C. Boyce a while later. "Let's go through it one more time. Are you absolutely positive this is the reporter's plaster rabbit?"

Gloria explained again how they'd all put their names on the rubber moulds. "And tomorrow when everything's been painted and decorated, we'll stick the paper with our names on underneath the bunnies and eggs ready for the competition next day."

"Right," said the policeman. "And, Janet, are you sure you saw the reporter outside her ladyship's rooms?"

Janet nodded. "I told Gloria earlier he looked flustered. I thought that was just because he felt a twerp, like I did for getting lost."

"But I bet it was because he'd been into the rooms," said Bernard. "And taken the pendant," he added. "And when he yelled at me for disturbing him when I took him some sandwiches in the tack room where he'd gone to take photographs of old saddles, I'm sure I saw a rubber mould on the bench.

"I thought he'd taken it in there to make sure nobody else could use it because he wanted to make a plaster rabbit. But I bet he'd filled it with wet plaster already and he'd gone to the tack room to bury the pendant in the plaster."

"It doesn't make sense," Janet said. "He'd surely be decorating and painting his plaster rabbit tomorrow, else somebody would notice if he and his rabbit wasn't there. They'd think it strange he'd gone when he's meant to be reporting the whole thing. Same goes for the next day when the judging takes place as well. He'd have to be there still.

"So how and when was he going to get the rabbit away with him? They're all going on a stall to be sold after the prizes have been awarded."

"That's easy," Gloria said. "He'd have bought his rabbit off the stall. I told Mum this morning there'd be a few of us buying our own egg or rabbit. Jeremy would have just taken his with him when he leaves."

"I bet her ladyship will get a right shock when she finds out her egg pendant is missing," said Bernard.

"We won't be sure of that, Bernard, until your dad gets back."

Gloria couldn't help smiling when she thought of the look on her dad's face when he'd arrived home just after Policeman Ken had got here and seen and heard what was going on.

It was her dad who'd suggested that he should go and have a private word with her ladyship – ask her to go and see *if* her pendant was missing. "Nobody will think anything of me needing to see her," he'd said. "If you or another policeman go, Ken, it might alert the thief. That's if there is a thief."

It was a little while before Gloria's dad returned. "Well?" she demanded, the second he walked in.

"It's a rum story, Ken," he said, looking at the policeman before pointing to the cellophane package on the work top. "Seems like this here pendant was replaced by a look-alike one. Her ladyship said it wasn't until she examined it really closely that she realised it wasn't hers but a fake one. A copy."

"I bet someone used the photograph of it that I saw in a magazine to make a fake one," said Gloria. "It was..."

"Never mind all that, Gloria," said Bernard. "What I want to know is how you're going to prove anything, Policeman Ken? That reporter won't be taking the pendant away inside his plaster bunny because the pendant is here."

"That's another thing, Ken," said Gloria's dad. "Her ladyship realised she never asked which magazine the reporter was from. Not even when he was taking photographs of her and her Russian egg jewellery. So happen he isn't really a reporter at all."

"Just a crook who saw the big advertisement for the Fun Day in one of the newspapers and thought he'd pretend to be a reporter," said Gloria. "And her ladyship fell for it when he phoned to ask if he could come and take photos and do a write-up."

"But we need to prove he's a crook," Bernard said.

"Do you know how long he's meant to be staying, Bill?" Policeman Ken asked him.

"I was to be taking him to the train station to catch the six o'clock train on Thursday."

"You're good at solving crimes and stuff, our Gloria," said Bernard. "Can't you think of some way we can still catch Jeremy red-handed?"

"It's lucky the barn's locked and I've got the only spare key," said Gloria. "Because I *have* got an idea."

"Thought you would have." Policeman Ken smiled at her. "Let's hear it and see if it's the same as mine. And, needless to say, not one single word of this must go any further," he added.

Bernard made a zipping motion across his lips and then drew a cross over his heart with his fingers.

*

Gloria yawned as, early the next morning, she unlocked the barn doors.

Once inside, she checked everything was as she and Policeman Ken had left it at gone midnight when they'd come up here with the rubber mould filled not only with plaster but with the egg pendant inside its cellophane packet as well.

And, late though it had been, she'd remembered to put the piece of paper with Jeremy's name on back on the mould.

Apart from her ladyship, Gloria was the only one with a key to the padlock, but a policeman had stayed hidden in the shadows all night in case of a break-in. So, really, she'd known everything would be as it should, thought Gloria, as she put out little tins of paint, paste, coloured paper and varnish ready for everyone to paint and decorate their egg or Easter bunny.

Now, they'd have to wait and hope the next part of the plan worked well.

It wasn't long before the prefab villagers – children and parents – arrived in the barn, followed shortly after, Gloria heaved a sigh of relief, by Jeremy.

But she felt herself trembling with nerves as she watched Jeremy starting to release his plaster bunny from its mould. Would the plaster she'd poured into it late last night be set? Would the bunny be in one piece? Had they buried the cellophane package deep enough in the plaster?

She needn't have worried. Jeremy's bunny turned out perfectly. And, she was so pleased to see, everyone else's had worked, too.

The smallest children – Janet's baby sister, Mary Clayton's little lad and one or two other of the younger kiddies, squealed in delight.

"They're so excited, bless them," said Mary Clayton, looking up from decorating her paper mâché egg.

But they were even more excited when an hour or so later, when they were all busily painting their bunnies, a large bunny on two legs walked into the barn.

"I'm the Easter Rabbit and I've come to give you all a chocolate egg to eat on Easter day," he said in a deep voice.

"He isn't real," said one of the children. "It's somebody dressed up."

Gloria stared hard at the bunny. She'd borrowed his costume from Maisie Butterworth who'd made a few such outfits to sell on her market stall. *Nobody*, Gloria thought, *will guess the Easter Rabbit is Policeman Ken*.

It had been her idea to dress him up to give out the chocolate eggs her ladyship had said she was providing. It would make it easy for him to keep an eye on Jeremy without Jeremy realising. And, of course, on the bunny with the valuable egg pendant hidden inside.

"We're having a picnic in her ladyship's walled garden when everybody has finished decorating and painting," Gloria said to the little ones. "Shall we ask the Easter Rabbit to stay for it?"

As she'd expected, they all shouted yes.

And, as they'd planned, Bernard, who was staying close to Jeremy, grinned up at him and said, "I bet that'll make a good photograph for your magazine. All of us at the picnic with a big Easter Rabbit. And the actor off that television programme should be here by then as well."

So Jeremy had no way of going off with his rabbit if he'd been planning to, because once everyone had gone to the walled garden for the picnic, Gloria locked the barn doors before joining them.

Though tomorrow will be harder than it's been today, she thought, walking home at the end of the day. We'll have to be extra alert to make sure Jeremy doesn't disappear after the judging.

*

Gloria was surprised at how quickly the time seemed to pass the next day.

As she'd guessed, after the judging of decorated eggs and bunnies, Jeremy had said he wanted to buy the one he'd made.

She'd told him that was OK and said he could collect it at home time because they'd put it out on the stall with a sold sticker on as that would encourage other folk to buy.

Policeman Ken, in his rabbit costume again, served on the stall with Gloria. The advertisements had done their job; there were a lot of people here. Now and then she caught sight of Jeremy taking photographs of them.

Although helping guard Jeremy's bunny meant she couldn't go and watch the performances, Gloria could hear everything.

Later in the afternoon, when the performances were over, people started leaving.

Gloria felt panicky when Jeremy came to fetch his bunny. But it was all right. Her dad arrived and told Jeremy he was ready to drive him to the station.

*

"It went like clockwork," Gloria's dad reported later to her, Janet and Bernard.

"Jeremy didn't suspect anything when I said I was giving the Easter Rabbit a lift. As planned I drove fast so Jeremy couldn't get out when Ken revealed his true identity and asked to see the plaster rabbit.

"Even before Ken cracked it open, Jeremy was burbling his confession."

"Then you drove to the police station?" Bernard said.

"I did, lad. Now I'm off up to the hall to report to her ladyship and your mum who's up there with her."

"Tell Tai-Lu's owner I'll take a lot of herring roes up in the morning," said Gloria. "Because if Tai-Lu hadn't knocked over Jeremy's bunny mould, her ladyship's genuine egg pendant would've vanished."

"And that horrid Jeremy would have got away with a clever crime," added Bernard.

Acknowledgements

Some of these prefab village stories made their first outing on the pages of The People's Friend magazines. A special thank you to David Young who illustrated those stories and brought the characters alive for me and everyone who read about them. He just had to be my choice for the cover artwork!

Massive thanks to Jo Bartlett and all at Fabrian Books for their help and advice.

To everyone who asked for more Broome Park Prefab Village stories: I hope you enjoy this Collection.

Also available from Pat Posner

Christmas Wishes… New Year Kisses

From their very first meeting, sparks fly between Rose and Matthew. Discovering they have a lot in common – they are both coping with loss and both have a parentless child to love and care for – sometimes calms things and sometimes ignites those sparks further as they lend each other moral support through tough times. And though they both wish there could be a relationship between them, there are reasons there can't be.

It doesn't help that they're thrown together when their little nieces become best friends and want to see a lot of each other. There's fun and laughter and silly happenings when they spend time together. Neither Rose nor Matthew can they deny the little girls something that so clearly helps them – especially as Christmas is drawing near and memories can be painful.

But Christmas is a time for making wishes. But how can Christmas wishes come true for Rose and Matthew and the two little best friends?

Also available from Fabrian Books

Cobblestone Cove and other stories

By Zara Thorne

This is a collection of thirteen short stories, most of which were previously published in The People's Friend magazine under the author's real name, Deirdre Palmer.

The characters you will meet are of all ages and backgrounds, each with their own way of seeing the world and dealing with its dilemmas. Take a trip back in time to the 1930's when fourteen-year-old Stella agonises over her first love, and to the 1960's when single mum Lizzie comes face-to-face with her past on a Bank Holiday trip to Brighton.

Back in the present day, young Molly finds the strength to face her problems in, of all places, a garden centre. It takes a trip to the Troodos mountains in Cyprus to restore Carl's faith in life; Paloma finds the path to her future in a seaside village in Devon, while the residents of exclusive Ivory Park are dismayed to find that high walls and security gates are no protection against petty crime.

Coffee-break, commute, beach or fireside – your quick read is here. Dip in and enjoy.

Saving Mr Scrooge

By Sharon Booth

How do you show the meanest man in the village the error of his ways?

It's the time of peace on earth and goodwill to all men, but at Carroll's Confectionary, the meaning of Christmas seems to have been forgotten. New boss, Kit Carroll, is hardly winning friends with his high-handed attitude, his foolhardy approach to production, and his tight-fisted treatment of the factory's employees.

Marley Jacobs, his self-styled PA, is determined to make him see the error of his ways, and return the festive spirit to Carroll's Confectionary.

Unfortunately, the little matter of their previous relationship, along with Kit's callous treatment of her when they were teenage sweethearts, keeps getting in the way of her good intentions.

With encouragement from co-worker Don, romantic sister Olivia, and — astonishingly — the usually sceptical Great Uncle Charles, Marley decides to save this modern-day Mr Scrooge from himself, despite having no well-meaning ghosts to help her.

But revisiting the past doesn't just stir things up for Kit. As Marley struggles to deal with bittersweet memories, present-day events take a surprising turn. Can the future be changed, after all? And is it only Kit who needs saving?

A Song for St Nicholas

By Jo Bartlett

Anna Byron is supposed to be living the dream. With a six figure salary and a boyfriend hinting at a Christmas proposal, it should be the perfect end to the year. Except Anna's life has never felt so empty and a chance encounter makes her realise it's time to go home to the beautiful seaside town of St Nicholas Bay.

Jamie Harrington was eighteen the last time he saw Anna, when he disappeared from her life without explanation; but ten years later he's back in the Bay, too, as the newly appointed vicar.

Setting up a Christmas choir seems like the perfect opportunity for them to give their relationship a second chance, but there are tensions in the group and secrets from the past soon start to unravel.

Someone's out to get the Harrington family and rumours about who was really involved in a tragic drowning a decade earlier won't go away. Weighed down by guilt, Jamie convinces himself that he doesn't deserve Anna's love and it looks like history - and his disappearing act - are about to repeat themselves.

Can Anna and Jamie let go of the past and learn to trust each other again or will the choir be disbanded for good by the time Christmas Eve comes around?

Available soon from Fabrian Books

Shadowed Love

By Pat Posner

Rissa loves her home in the North Yorkshire dale of Hebbledale. But it bruises her teenage heart when Logan, her brother's best friend and the man she worships tells her there's someone special in his life, adding that there are reasons he can't tell her how he feels. However, that doesn't change how Rissa feels about Logan and even though the violets he gave her to pin on her dress for the Valentine's Dance were clearly nothing but a kind and 'big brotherly' gesture, she presses them so they'll last for ever.

When Rissa is in her twenties, her brother is killed in an accident. Soon after, Rissa learns the person Logan is in love with is her newly widowed sister-in-law.

Shocked, angry and disillusioned, Rissa leaves Hebbledale and her only remaining family.

Four years later, when her sister-in-law is taken to hospital, Rissa is called home to look after her little niece. Rissa is distraught when she finds out how wrong she's been about Logan. But he's living in Ireland now; he's someone from her past, and she is engaged to Justin.

When her niece makes a surprising discovery, Rissa's secret doubts about Justin are confirmed. Then Logan returns and Rissa knows that, like the violets, her love for him has never faded. But it's clear he still sees her as a sort of sister. Isn't it...?

Printed in Great Britain
by Amazon

34603512R00087